The Threads of Fate

An enchanted quill's retelling of the Boy Who Lived

Clever Fox® PUBLISHING
Chennai • Bangalore

CLEVER FOX PUBLISHING
Chennai, India

Published by CLEVER FOX PUBLISHING 2025

ISBN: 978-93-6707-219-6

DEDICATION

To my dear friends, Rithika and Shivika.D—
thank you for standing by me,
inspiring me,
and sharing in the magic of this journey.
Your love for Harry Potter and your support in writing this story made every page possible.

Chapter-1---

It was a humid atmosphere in the wizarding world. With temperatures going up to 38-degree Fahrenheit and 51-degree Fahrenheit. Among this warm and tropical climate, there was one boy who was shivering under his blankets. While the rest of the townsfolk were sweating profusely due to the heat, Harry Potter was shuddering. He heard an owl hoot outside and woke up with a start, perspiring more than ever. “What’s the matter?” his friend Ron asked from the nearby bed. “Are you alright?” “Yes. I’m fine” he replied. “Just a nightmare.” “Harry” Ron cried “You need to stop having nightmares. The battle is already over. You can’t revive the dead.” “Well, what do I do to stop having nightmares? “Take occlumency lessons from Snape or what?” he yelled. But then, Harry instantly regretted it. Ron’s face started to drain color. “Let me sleep, Ron. Just wanna sleep.” “Sure, mate” he replied, “Call me if you need anything.” Harry nodded. He couldn’t muster the courage to say anything more. He had just spoken about Snape. Severus Snape, the potions master, who he despised a lot and was a death eater, turned out to be the one to love Lily Potter unconditionally. He cherished Lily, so much that his Patronus took her form- a doe. But now, there was no use thinking about this, Harry said to himself. After the battle of Hogwarts, about a month, Harry was living with the Weasleys at their home- The Burrow. Harry couldn't think of going to his godfather's house or his parents' house, because there was no one left for him. All his family, died before him, beginning with Lily and James Potter, Sirius Black, The wisest headmaster- Albus Dumbledore, Hedwig (his snowy white owl), Dobby (The only elf who trusted him unconditionally), Fred Weasley, Remus Lupin (his father's friend), Nymphadora Tonks and finally Severus Snape. The deaths of all these people haunted Harry in such a way that he was forced to relive these moments in his dreams causing him to shiver. Why was all this happening to him? Why can't someone else withstand the worst of this torture? But no, it had to be Harry, because he was "THE CHOSEN ONE." Voldemort marked Harry Potter as his equal and gave him the scar. The CHOSEN ONE could also have been Neville, as he was also born at the end of July. But no. Voldemort had to choose him; he viewed Harry as his greatest threat and danger. He was the cause of all the deaths, all the trauma which Harry had to bear. Harry gently traced the scar on his head. He had gotten it 19 years ago, when he was about to be killed and Lily Potter cast herself between them. He had also recently discovered that he had been a horcrux, and that he was the Master of the Deathly Hallows. He owned his father's invisible cloak; he used the Resurrection Stone and the Elder Wand answered to him. In spite, of being the Master of Death, he couldn't save anyone. Anyone. He missed Fred's laughter, the flirty banter between Remus and Tonks, Colin's small frame which didn't belong among the dead bodies. He had expected light emerging from the dark clouds after the battle, but the darkness spread through him. He silently wished, he could have died that day along with the others- into peace, into oblivion. The guilt of everyone's death was spreading through Harry. Not thinking about anything, further, he wrapped himself in his blankets and fell asleep into temporary tranquility and peace...

Chapter-2-------

"Harry, Wake up. It's time for breakfast. Come on Harry!" he heard Hermione's voice waking him up. He awoke and grabbed his glasses from the nearby table. "Sorry, Harry. I would have let you sleep, but Mrs. Weasley insisted that I wake you up as soon as possible Hermione apologized. "It's alright. I'm fine. Where's Ron?" he looked over at his nearby bed. "Ron's gone to remove some gnomes from the garden along with George ". Harry's heart ached. The last time he had uprooted gnomes was with Fred and George together. George's life has become incomplete without Fred. Every mirror in the house seemed to be covered and hidden, Ginny had told him the reason once. "George doesn't want to see any reflection of himself, because it reminded him of Fred." How was Harry ever to console George about what happened to Fred. He couldn't even produce a Patronus after seeing his twin die. He had lost his closest companion, partner in pranks and the person he had shared his entire life with. His grief was much more than Harry's guilt. Mrs. Weasley- who had looked after Harry like her own son; how was Harry ever going to apologize to her about what he did to Fred, how he was responsible for all their deaths. The house felt emptier and quiet. Hermione, sensing the shift in his demeanor said, “Come on, freshen up and let’s go down.” Harry nodded. Again, he was speechless about what to say. He quickly freshened up and went down. Mrs. Weasley was waiting for him. “Ah there you are dear” she said. Even though she was physically more active than before, but mentally she was drained out. Her voice had a lack of cheerfulness and authority since Fred passed away. Her hands trembled with the crockery. The family clock remained untouched on the wall, unbearable to look at. Harry often saw her knitting at night, sitting by the fire trying to distract herself from her son’s death. When she hugged him, he could feel her grip tighter, as if she was afraid, he might vanish too. Though she spoke happily, there was a huge void in her empty heart. “There was a letter addressed to you. Errol brought it over here.” She gestured to a ruddy brown owl with ruffled feathers. Harry was curious. Who would address letters to him now? What if they were admirers saying how well he performed in the battle? Or was the Ministry of Magic, congratulating him on something. He hoped not. Perhaps it could be from Hagrid or Neville. He took the letter from Errol’s beak, and the owl gently nibbled his finger. He turned it over and saw the Hogwarts School of Witchcraft and Wizardry symbol on it. He was left gaping. Maybe they were insisting him, to complete his final year, he thought. He tore open the letter and read it aloud.

Dear Mr. Potter,

Hope you're alright. I've a piece of news to give you. I was arranging the headmistress study when I noticed a letter addressed to you, from Professor Dumbledore. I was wondering if you could come around to have a chat and open the letter.

Yours sincerely,

Minerva McGonagall

Headmistress

Harry was shocked. He was unable to think anything. His brain began picking out every single word and finally joined it to form a single sentence. He didn't expect this to happen. That too, a letter from Dumbledore made matters worse for him. What would the letter be about? Is it a secret about Harry's parents or worse about Voldemort? He couldn't bear any more secrets. The battle was over, and he blamed himself for every single one who died. They all died for him. Tears started welling in his eyes. He felt a hand on his shoulder and turned around to face Molly Weasley. "I'll have the floo powder ready for you, Harry. You can go and be back. And give Professor McGonagall my regards." He pulled Mrs. Weasley into a hug and said "Thank you, Mrs. Weasley. Thank you for everything." She just nodded and tears began to form in her eyes. But she held everything together, all her feelings were bottled up inside her, for the welfare of the rest of the family. "You are like my son, Harry. I don't expect a thank you from you." Harry began crying. She gently patted his head and left his grip to get the floo powder. "Here you go" she came back in a moment or two carrying the greenish powder. "Remember, be loud and clear." Harry gulped and went inside the fireplace. He had unbelievably bad experiences with Floo Powder. He dropped the floo powder on the ground and said "Hogwarts Headmistress Study ". The very next second, he felt himself being pulled into the familiar, disorienting sensation and opened his eyes to find a lady wearing green robes, her hair tied back in a high bun staring at him. "My word, Mr. Potter. You should have informed me prior about your arrival. I was going to turn you into something horrible." "Sorry Professor. I mean Headmistress." "Its fine" McGonagall said, "I wasn't expecting your arrival instantly." "I thought it would be something important, that is why, I came Professor." "Have a seat, Potter. I'll bring the letter." Harry sat down in front of the Headmistress chair. The office was exactly the same except for Dumbledore's portrait waving from the top middle area. The sword of Godric Gryffindor was resting in its glass case. The Sorting Hat sitting drowsily on the shelf. And Fawkes, the phoenix's cage empty and worn out. Everything else was the same, the pensive, the vials, the wonky instruments. His thoughts were interrupted by the stamping of boots as McGonagall came into view. "Professor, why isn't Snape's portrait on the wall?" The guilt almost choked Harry on asking a question like that. He himself was shocked by the question which came from his mouth. "Professor Snape" corrected McGonagall. "Yes, Professor Snape." "Well," she began "It is being prepared currently as we speak." After a few moments of silence, her face became softer and gentle. She said "Potter, Are you alright?" Harry wasn't sure whether to tell her the truth. He could tell

Dumbledore, but he wasn't there in mortal form, only as a portrait. "I'm fine, Professor." "Good. Now," she said handing over the letter "I want you to open it in front of me and read it aloud. Harry nodded his head. He opened the letter, and his eyes began to water because of the familiar handwriting. Tears began clouding his vision, but he blinked it aside and read.

Harry,

If you're reading this, then it means, I probably am dead. But I want you to stay brave and not cry. I am writing this letter to inform you of something incredibly important and unofficial. While I was reading my old books in my office, I found a book on "THE DEPARTMENT OF MYSTERIES ". I thought of reading it; hence I sat down to read it. It was a thrilling book, and it talked about many prophecies and predictions. But the one that caught my eye was in Row. No 17. That was the only one which did not mention anything. Even in your prophecy Row. No. 97, the forecast was written. It intrigued me. I thought it was a weapon for fighting against the Dark Lord. Hence, I tried tracing the author, to find exactly what was written. But the author was no more. Gradually, I forgot about the prophecy and the row and abandoned my quest. One day, it came into my mind, and I noted it down for you. Cause there was no guarantee whether I would live that long. If you're reading this, I would recommend you have a look. It might not be addressed to you, but it doesn't hurt to have a look.

Sincerely.

Albus Dumbledore.

Now, Harry couldn't stop tears from coming into his eyes. He wiped it with his sleeve and looked at McGonagall. She was unsure about what to say. She let the silence settle in. "We need to go there" she said. "This might be Albus's last wish. We need fulfill it." "Harry" she turned looking at him "Will Molly be expecting you now?" "No, Professor. I don't think so." "Are you willing to come?" Her voice was calm yet stern. "Yes Professor." "Alright. We'll take the Floo Network."

Chapter -3----

"Department of Mysteries" announced the audio. The lifts opened to reveal the same highly secretive division of the Ministry of Magic, shrouded in secrecy, and dedicated to research on the deepest mysteries of the wizarding world, such as love, death, time, and space. Harry led the way as he had been here before. They stepped out of the lift into the black, tiled, circular room. This enchanted room spins whenever a door closes, making it difficult to track the whereabouts of a specific room. He opened the door ahead of him and saw himself facing the 'Death Chamber'- A stone amphitheater with a stone archway that holds the Veil. Harry immediately closed the door. He felt sick, not because of the current spinning of the room but of the place. That is the place, where Sirius died. That is the place where Bellatrix killed him. The exact place where his only family member was taken away from him by the cruel threads of fate. McGonagall placed a hand on his shoulder "Harry, we need to focus please." Harry nodded. He couldn't do anything except nod. He opened the next door and found what he required- 'The Hall of Prophecy' a room with soaring ceilings and thousands of glass orbs stacked in shelves. “Lumos” he muttered. Knowing what to do, as he had been here before, searching for his own prophecy, he walked past the orbs, directly to Row 17. “This one” he said to McGonagall. She nodded and brought her wand close to read the name on it. But there was no name given, only a title. “It is strange” muttered McGonagall. “Sorry Professor. But what is strange?” “Every prophecy has a name Harry. To whom it was destined to. But this one doesn’t have any name. It’s odd. Without a name, it’s considered to be false. But the unspeakables, ensure that no false prediction can make their way here.” “How do we know what the prophecy is, Professor?” “I thought you know this already. We hold it” saying so she held the dusty glass orbs in her hands. At first, the voice was distorted. Then it became clearer. Finally, Harry could make out what it said.

Born under the shadow of war, raised by those who defy the Dark Lord, a child has emerged—hailed by many as the one foretold. Even the Dark Lord himself has taken notice, marking the child as his greatest threat. But he is wrong. The one he fears... is not the one he should. What he has seen is only a carefully woven illusion—a decoy crafted to deceive. Somewhere, hidden in the far corners of the wizarding world, the true Chosen One lives in obscurity. Unaware. Unawakened. And when their time comes... the world will never be the same.

McGonagall looked at Harry. "Professor. What does this mean?" Harry asked still not understanding. McGonagall looked stunned. Harry had seen her for the first time out of words. "Professor" Harry tried again. She was shocked. She kept mumbling to herself in disbelief. Regaining her composure barely she replied, "It means that you're not the chosen one and the real chosen one lies unaware of their identity." "So, it's not me?!" Harry was flabbergasted. All his life, ever since he stepped into the Wizarding World, he was famous. Everyone knew him. Because he was 'THE CHOSEN ONE.' The 'ONE' whom Voldemort has marked as his equal. The 'ONE' whose parents were killed by Voldemort. The 'ONE' whom Voldemort; the greatest dark wizard of all time could never kill. "What about Trelawney's prediction? What about...?" "I don't know the answers to your questions, Potter. And I'm also not the right person to give you answers." "Then who is the right person, Professor? The only one who could give me answers is DEAD! And I saw him dying, yet I couldn't save him!" Harry crumpled onto the floor. He just wanted to escape this life. He wanted to be normal. He would trade everything, only if he could become a MUGGLE and not a WIZARD. “Harry. Please compose yourself.” McGonagall consoled him. “He cast a full-body-bind curse on you. There was nothing you could do. Dumbledore only wanted to protect you. It’s not your fault. Don’t blame yourself for the deaths of everyone. Albus wouldn’t have wanted that.” Harry felt truth in her words. It’s not like he could do anything when Dumbledore died. It was futile to sit here crying rather than finding out what the unknown prophecy was about. “You’re right, Professor” he said standing up. “Professor Dumbledore didn’t sacrifice his life, for me to sit and cry. And Sirius also used to say, ‘The ones that love us never really leave us.’ What do we do about the prophecy, Professor?” McGonagall gave one of her rare smiles. “I’m not exactly sure, Potter. But if you’re not the one chosen, it must be someone else. Why don’t you do one thing? Go and talk to Mr. Malfoy.” Harry couldn’t believe his ears. McGonagall was asking him to go and talk to Draco Malfoy, his bully, his arch nemesis? But he had changed. After all, Draco wasn’t the one to kill Dumbledore. A mutual understanding did exist between both after the battle, but they never spoke to each other. “Professor, why Malfoy?” “Clearly, it’s because Draco was a DEATH EATER in our school. And despite being an ally of Voldemort, he refused to kill Dumbledore and didn’t you tell me, that in Malfoy Manor, Draco pretended not to recognize you. It means that he doesn’t want to go to DARK side. Just go and have a chat with him, listen to his views and perspectives about Voldemort. He might know things which we don’t after being his supporter. “Alright Professor. But Mrs. Weasley might be waiting for me. I haven’t had breakfast yet.” “That’s not a problem. I’ll send an owl to her, letting her know that you’re out with me. Go now, Potter. I need to examine this prophecy.” Harry nodded and turned out. He walked out of THE DEPARTMENT OF MYSTERIES and took the lift to the reception. There, he once again went inside fireplace, shut his eyes, and said “MALFOY MANOR!”

Chapter-4----

He opened his eyes and walked a few steps from the fireplace to see a tall, large manor, located in the countryside, in an area surrounded by high stone walls, providing privacy and seclusion which reflects the pure-blood status of their family. The last time Harry was here, he was being held as a prisoner in the dungeons along with Ron, while Hermione was being tortured by Bellatrix Lestrange. His jaw clenched when that name came to his mind. She killed Sirius Black, Tonks and used the 'Cruciatus Curse' on Neville's parents, due to which they were in St. Mungo's Hospital right now. He reached the front door. A large serpent-shaped emerald knocker was awaiting him. He knocked on the door and waited. After a few moments, he heard footsteps coming towards the door. The door opened and Harry saw the familiar blond hair; pale skin and the ones-cold eyes shone with excitement on seeing him. "Hi, Draco" Harry said awkwardly. Draco held his hand, pulled him inside and gave him a hug. Harry almost fell down due to the bone-crushing hug. When Draco finally let go of him, his eyes were brimming with tears. Harry didn't know what to say. "I'm so sorry, Potter" he erupted. "I shouldn't have allied with The Dark

Lord. I didn't know he was going to ask me to kill Dumbledore. I swear. My father insisted that I maintain our honor by serving the Dark Lord as our family has done for centuries." "Sit down Draco" Harry said prompting him to the sofa. Draco nodded. "It's alright, Draco. What you did was under pressure. I can understand." "Forgive me Potter please. I beg you!" He started crying even more. "I forgive you, Draco. I really do." That seemed to make him stop crying. "Why are you here? I wanted to speak to you, but I didn't know whether you would like to meet me" Draco said. "I wanted your help." "Sure, anything. Tell me what it is." So, Harry told him everything about the prophecy. How the prophecy mentioned that he's not the chosen one. "Do you know anyone who could be the actual chosen one?" Harry enquired. "No, in fact I'm quite astounded by this prophecy." "Well," Harry said "Mostly, I came to have a chat with you. I want to know your opinion on Voldemort." Harry wished he hadn't said that as Draco's eyes started brimming with tears again. "Well, I'm glad someone came to enquire about me. My father, whom I used to consider as my everything, kept a big secret from me. I-I-I-I ..." he stuttered and cried. "It's alright, Draco, if you don't want to tell me no problem." "Its fine"

Draco said, blowing his nose "I must tell someone. I-I-I used to have a sister." Harry fell out of the chair in shock. Draco Malfoy, having a sister. No way. His heart froze. At first, Harry thought he was blabbering something just to humiliate and sneer at him. But the pained look in his eyes, spoke countless words. Harry felt a strange twist inside him. Indeed, he couldn't imagine Draco having a sibling. He couldn't picture anyone owning the 'Malfoy' name other than his sneering and potentially dangerous rival who was weeping in front of him. If she had a sister, where is she? Why hadn't anyone spoken about her? A sister meant- another life tangled into Draco's. Another soul possessing the 'Malfoy' honor and reputation. And though he hated to admit it, there was a flicker of sympathy within it. He knew how it was to be separated from one's family and secrets being kept from him. "I know it's unbelievable" he continued "Even I couldn't believe it at first, but my mother is sick. So, when, I went to her room to console her, she told me that I had a sister- Drea Malfoy. She was only a baby when father left her in Knockturn Alley." He wept and howled, in a way that the loss of his sister hurt his soul "He left her because, he didn't want a girl child in our family. I was only 3 years old. I don't even remember." He was bawling. Harry quickly got up and put a hand on his shoulder." I didn't know. I'm sorry." Just then, someone came walking down the stairs. "Draco," the voice said, "Who're you talking to"? Harry knew that icy, cold voice very well. He even knew the person who owned that voice. Draco instantly got up from his seat. He beckoned Harry towards the door. "Go" he said "If Father, sees you, he'll kill you. Go" Harry turned to go. "Pottah" Draco's pained voice said, "Don't tell this to anyone." Harry nodded and ran towards the fireplace where he'd come from.

Chapter-5-----

" Wow" said Ron unable to say anything more. Harry had travelled through the Floo Network once more and landed in the Burrow where Mrs. Weasley overfed him. Finally, with a bloated stomach, he could talk to Ron and Hermione in their room. Hermione didn't utter a single word throughout the conversation. She was deep in thought. "But Harry the prophecy..." "Who gives a damn about the prophecy. Draco has a sister!?" Ron interrupted. "Sssshhh, Ron" Harry yelled. "Wow, who would believe that ferret has a sister." "Well, that's not our concern, whatever happened to his sister. Our concern is the prophecy. Who else could be the chosen one?" "Well, Hermione" Harry was about to say but Ginny opened the door and came in. "Phew I'm so tired. Mum made me scrub the whole kitchen without magic. Can you imagine? Oh, Hi Harry!" "Hi Ginny" he replied. Ron, Hermione exchanged continuous glances at Harry, begging him silently to change the topic. "So", Ginny said "I've heard George's joke shop is going quite well." Harry was glad that she herself changed the topic, but he wished for a better change. Fred and George's Joke Shop- Weasley's Wizard Wheezes situated in Diagon Alley which sells pygmy puffs, extendable ears, skiving snack boxes and all the joke stuff the twins could think of. The money for the shop was given by Harry to them, after he earned his winnings. “George’s not feeling good these days.” Ginny continued. Oh-no-no thought Harry. Not about Fred and George please. “I’ve just been to see him. He doesn’t want anything. He was crying on my shoulder and not letting me go.” Ginny said, her eyes were watering. Harry wanted to rub those tears out of his eyes. He never wanted to see Ginny crying. Maybe he had some unknown feelings for her. He controlled himself. He suddenly got reminded of Hagrid. “Hagrid,” Harry said, “How’s he?” “He’s most probably fine. Nothing must have happened to him,” said Ginny. “Ginny” Mrs. Weasley’s voice came through the room “Come down, right now.” “She probably has more work to give me” said Ginny as she rolled her eyes and went down into the kitchen. A few moments later she came up with a piece of parchment rolled in her hand. “Who’s it for?” said Ron, eyeing the parchment wearily. “For Harry.” Harry was going to snatch the parchment from her when she pulled it back. “I’ll give you the parchment, Harry, but tell me what is going on?” “Fine, Ginny. I’ll tell you. Give me the parchment now.” Suspiciously, she handed Harry the parchment. He unfurled it and read it. He handed it over to Hermione's outstretched hand, a look of awe and shock on his face. Hermione read it aloud—

Dear Mr. Potter,

I examined the prophecy and even tried to find the owner of it as Prof. Dumbledore said. I inspected his study, to see if any more information was available. It seems to have been written by Oswald Godwin Longbottom. The great-grandfather of your friend Neville Longbottom. Although I couldn't find anything else, I suggest you pay Neville a visit. And I hope to hear what Malfoy said too. I'll be expecting you tomorrow morning. Bring, Mr. Weasley and his sister, Ms. Granger. Mr. Malfoy and Mr. Longbottom.

Regards,

Minerva McGonagall

Headmistress

"Well," said Ginny "Can someone tell me, what is going on? Why has McGonagall called me and Neville? And what prophecy again?" Harry indicated for Hermione to narrate the story. Hermione took a deep breath and began the tale while Harry watched Ginny's expression morph from calm and collected to astonished, shocked. "So, he's not the chosen one?" "According to the prophecy, he isn't," said Hermione. "Can we go to meet Neville tomorrow? It's almost night" whined Ron impatiently. "Honestly, Ron. McGonagall will be expecting us tomorrow morning, which means we must go now." said Hermione. "Would Mum allow?" Ron asked Ginny. "Only if we inform her and go" she said. "Let's go then," said Harry.

Chapter-6----

Harry found himself facing Oakshade Manor. Unlike Malfoy's house, this manor looked pleasant and inviting. The gardens appeared to be older than the house itself, thick with enchanted oaks that swayed and whispered in the wind. "I didn't know, this was Neville's house," said Ron. "Harry, his grandma will be there. What do we tell her?" "Say the truth. That we're here to meet Neville" replied Hermione. "What's the delay about? Let's go" snapped Ginny. Harry couldn't help wondering- she even looked cute when she was angry. Her bright red hair (a common trait of the Weasley family) began streaming in the wind. Her brown eyes portrayed her annoyance and anger. And her freckles began to stand apart, making her look captivating, dazzling Harry would say. "Let's go Harry" Hermione said as she nudged him from behind after Ron and her bickering. "Honestly, what does Ronald think of himself" ranted Hermione. "He's yelling at me because he wants to sleep, and we bought him here!" "YOU COULD HAVE LEFT ME!" Ron said from behind. "TO HAVE YOU WHINE LIKE A BABY WHEN WE GET BACK!!" Hermione argued. "ONCE AGAIN, YOU CALL ME A BABY HERMIONE, I'LL...!" "For god's sake, stop fighting both of you!" yelled Harry. "Harry's right," said Ginny. "Stop fighting. We're here to see Neville." "WHY ARE YOU SO INTERESTED IN SEEING NEVILLE!" yelled Ron again. "Harry" Ginny said addressing him "I can't tolerate Ron. Please do something." Harry felt a surge of pride and a small firecracker in his stomach. "Guys please, stop. We reached Neville's house." By the time they were arguing, all four of them reached the manor. A golden-yellowish house stood before them. The color was so bright, it looked like it would outshine the sun. Maybe Neville thought it would look like a sunflower, associating his love for nature. Ginny raised the brass knocker and knocked three times. The door opened almost instantly. A lady in around mid-60s or 70s wearing a vulture-topped hat and stiff old-fashioned clothes opened the door. Her look appeared to be stern, but when her eyes met Ginny's, they softened. "Hello, Ginny dear" Augusta Longbottom said. "How are you?" "I'm fine Gran. Is Neville here?" Ginny enquired. "Yes, he's doing something in his room. Ahh! And you must be Harry, Ron, and Hermione, isn't it?" "Correct, Gran" Ginny said, "Is it alright if we meet Neville?" "Sure, the poor boy would love some company." She opened the door wider, gestured them all to come inside. “Climb up the first flight of steps and the second door on your right.” “Thank you” said Harry and they began climbing the stairs. At the top of the stairs, Ron held Ginny’s hand “How does, Neville’s grandmother know you so well?” “Ron, we’re just friends” snapped Ginny. “You’re also friends with Hermione. Do I question your friendship with her?” Ron looked a bit shy and left his hold onto her. Hermione cleared her throat. Ron looked at Hermione and gave a slight smile. “Guys we’re here,” said Harry. There seemed to be lots of noise coming from Neville’s bedroom. Books falling, things cluttering and many more. Harry gave a slight knock and opened the door to find Neville dueling with a dummy. “Stupefy!” Neville yelled, out of breath and sweating “Reducto!” “Expelliarmus!” He stopped on seeing Harry, Ron, Ginny, and Hermione peeking behind the door. “Bloody Hell Neville! What is going on?” exclaimed Ron. “Nothing guys, have a seat. ‘Clarus Omnia’’ he muttered clearing all the mess that he’d created. “I didn’t expect you to be here. I desperately needed some company. I’ve missed you all” sniffled Neville. “It’s alright, Neville. We’re here now” consoled Harry. “Actually, Neville, we need your help” stated

Ginny. “What is it?” enquired Neville still sniffling. And so, Harry tells him the entire tale.

Chapter-7---

"No way!" exclaimed Neville. "My great-grandfather was the one who authored the book! Harry, why didn't you say this at the beginning of the story! There are a few scrolls, manuscripts and parchments preserved by him in our library along with my Herbology books. I'll take you there, right now." "Blimey, Neville. Don't you get bored of reading Herbology books?" questioned Ron. "Well," Neville looked sheepishly "I'm just interested in Herbology still." "Guys, can we please go to the library?" pleaded Ginny. "Yes, sure" said Harry as he led the way down the stairs. "Turn towards your right Harry" directed Neville as he was the last. "You will find a door, straight ahead. Enter it, go left, and turn again. You will find the library." Hermione went awestruck on seeing the library. "Wow, Neville!" she squealed "This is magnificent! It is my dream library! Oh my god! This is just indescribable!" Harry could clearly see why. In every place possible, there were bookshelves lined, each filled with almost a dozen books. Also, books were floating everywhere, neatly stacking themselves on the shelves. A towering, dome shaped ceiling enabled sunlight to set foot into the room, illuminating it. A few couches bordered the shelves along with tables. Various maps, herbology books and a globe was situated on one of the tables. As Harry was mesmerized by the whole scene, he heard Neville shout

"Accio!" and point his wand at a few dusty leather-bound books and parchments, which neatly settled themselves on the table. Hermione went haywire. She kept on walking around the shelves, glancing at books and muttering to herself. "Leave her" whispered Ron in his ear, "You know how she becomes around books. Let's see what Neville's got" saying so, he tugged Harry towards the table. "Here it is, Harry" said Neville handing over the books and the parchment. Harry opened it one-by-one and turned to a random page. "Why are words forming on their own, on the page?" Ginny asked. Harry closed the book as soon as she said it. "Oh, that's some random thing. A myth, to be precise." "What's it, Neville?" piped up Ron. "Well, cause my whole family is a pureblood, we used to use magic for almost everything. My great grandfather believed in the past and the future. So, in his books, he left a few pages empty, on which words would form about the people reading it, thus, predicting their future. But it's all a myth of course. "Have you ever tried it, Neville?" asked Harry. "No, I haven't even touched it. In fact, this book was gathering dust and spider webs over the years. No one opened it till now." "Well, then Harry, open it and go to any random page" insisted Ron. Harry sighed and opened the book to a random page. Words, like an invisible hand was writing them, began pouring all over the page. At first, it was indecipherable. Slowly. Slowly, it became readable. When it finally stopped, Ron, Neville and Ginny bent over Harry to look curiously. Harry found it too confused and was just blinking. Hermione, finally seeing the bewildered look on their faces, grabbed the book from Harry's hands and read it-

When scarred lies fade and truth is clear,

Six shall stand, united here.

Together bound by fate's own thread,

To seek the Codex long since dead.

Through fractured time and shadowed past,

They'll find the keys that hold it fast.

But one of fire, born to lead,

Shall claim the crown through word and deed.

No path alone can break the chain,

For only strength in hearts combined

Shall wake the power, forge the key,

And set the hidden spirit free.

"Hermione, what is this about?" questioned Ron. Ginny gave him a quizzical look, and then looked at Harry, who averted his eyes. Hermione was biting her lip. "I'm not exactly sure. But this is about THE CHOSEN ONE." "How do you know?" said Ron. Hermione rolled her eyes, and Ron went a bit pink. "The myth says that it predicts the reader's future, which is, OUR FUTURE and it's talking about a quest. That much is explicit." She thought for a moment, Ron couldn't help staring at her. "Neville, I saw a book on ancient spells. But I don't remember which shelf." "Not a problem" said Neville in a cheery voice, as he pointed his wand to a bookshelf and murmured "Accio!" The book flew from the shelf and landed neatly in Hermione's hands. She didn't waste a moment as she opened the book, referred to the index and flipped through pages. Finally, she raised her hands and clapped. "Of course, I was so stupid. The word 'codex' is just a fancy word for a book, scroll, or magical document — but in fantasy, it's usually something ancient, secret, and powerful" she concluded. "There's a drawing as well" pointed Ron as he brushed her hand, seemed to have stealthily moved behind Hermione. "Oh, ah yes" said Hermione, goosebumps developing at the point of contact. "This looks like a gem or something" stated Ginny from behind Harry. He turned and nodded. She smiled and blushed away. "Is the Codex, a weapon?" enquired Neville. "Presumably, yes" answered Hermione. “Ginny, what’s the time?” she questioned as the sunlight was being replaced by the moon. “It’s time for dinner!” she exclaimed. “Blimey! Mum will be so mad! Neville, I’m so sorry, mate. We got to go. Is there a fireplace in your house connected to the Floo Network?” grumbled Ron “Yes, there’s one in the library itself” said Neville, as he led them to the corner of the library, where they hadn’t seen the fireplace due to the bookshelves. “We better get going, Neville. I’ll send you an owl if we need you” added Harry hastily as he saw Neville’s sullen face. One by one, they walked into the fireplace and reached THE BURROW.

Chapter-8----

"Why are you so late?" Mrs. Weasley screamed at Ron and Ginny. "Mum, we just..." "Quiet Ron! Have you seen the time! I was so worried!! All of you have some toast. That's your punishment. I've left it on the table. I'll go and see George. And eat, and directly, go to bed!" Mrs. Weasley growled. They quietly finished their food and trotted upstairs. "What's wrong with Mum? She's always hysterical these days." Ron complained as soon as they shut the door. "Well, me and Hermione have to go to bed, otherwise Mum, would kill us. See you tomorrow, Harry. Good night" Ginny said as she and Hermione, wandered out of the room. No sooner, they wandered out of the room, Ron jumped to Harry's bed, "Harry, does Ginny like you?" Harry was taken aback by the question. "What! No! I don't think so." "She does! Haven't you seen the way she acknowledges you? She wished you 'Good Night' instead of me, I'm her brother." "Ron, Even I can say that you like Hermione!" "What no!" Ron stumbled onto the floor. "Then why do you keep staring at her?" Ron was speechless. He kept opening and closing his mouth like a goldfish. Finally, after several minutes, he found his voice again, "Good Night, Harry. We've to go and see McGonagall tomorrow as well." He switched off the lights, wrapped his Canon blanket around him and slept. Harry too decided to sleep, but thought of sending an owl to Draco, informing him of their arrival tomorrow. He grabbed some parchment and quill and began to write—

Draco,

Me, Ron, Hermione, Ginny, and Neville will be coming to your house tomorrow morning. McGonagall insists on seeing you and all of us. Don't inform anyone else about this. Also, don't plague your mind with Drea's thoughts.

Harry

He quietly went down to the kitchen, praying silently that he wouldn't find Mrs. Weasley. Luckily, she wasn't there. Harry went to Errol's cage. The ruddy brown owl was sleeping peacefully; when Harry prodded it lightly, it nibbled his fingers. He fastened the letter to Errol and let it go. He watched as Errol flew and flew and finally became a blur in the night sky.

Chapter-9-------

"Get up, Ron. Sleepy-head!" Hermione was continuously slapping him with the pillows. After Harry tried waking him up, which was an unsuccessful attempt, he had called Hermione. "I fell of my broom! I couldn't catch the snitch!" Ron suddenly started screaming as he woke up. "Shut up, Idiot! Get ready, quick. We've to meet McGonagall." Hermione warned sternly. As she was about to go, she turned and asked Harry "Did you see Ginny today morning?" "No, why?" Harry enquired. "She was not there, when I woke up." "She must have wandered somewhere" said Ron who finally awoke from his temporary sleep. "Last time, early morning, she'd gone somewhere, and Mum was so worried... She was about to faint when Ginny came. Mum asked her where she had been, and she just said she was roaming around for approximately 2 hours! She'll be back late, I believe. Anyway, let's go! Its already time!" "Should we get Neville and Draco?" Hermione asked. "Well off-course, Miss know it-all. McGonagall specified to get them both. Didn't she Harry?" Harry nodded. Hermione glared. They went down, informed Mrs. Weasley and travelled via the floo Network to Neville's house. "Hello, Dears" Mrs. Augusta Longbottom said. "Gran, Professor McGonagall wants to meet Neville and us. Could we take him along?" Hermione stated politely. Ron couldn't help staring at her. "Sure, I'll just call him.

Neville! Your friends are here to take you!" She started talking rapidly addressing them "He was continuously telling me yesterday, that you all would be coming to take him. He was really excited. Give McGonagall my regards. Such a strong lady, managing Hogwarts after everything happened. But she wasn't always like this you know. She used to be fragile, like a piece of glass, but now..." Luckily, she was interrupted by Neville, who came outside. "Ahh, Neville. Be a good boy. Don't embarrass yourself in front of McGonagall." Neville's ears went pink. "Yes Gran. I'll be back soon. Take care" saying so he and the others waved goodbye and walked towards the fireplace where they had come from. "Bloody Hell, does your grandma always talks this much, Neville?" Neville nodded. Next, they went to Malfoy Manor, to get to Draco. "Shouldn't we inform him of our arrival beforehand?" Hermione asked. "I had already sent him a letter yesterday, informing him that we would be arriving." Harry said. "What if his father opens the door?" Neville asked trembling. "Nothing will happen, Neville. Draco will take care of it." Harry patted Neville on the back, and they began the walk towards the house. Harry could see the look of recognition and a bit of fear on Ron and Hermione's face, both recalling their last encounter with this place. Harry raised and knocked on the emerald-green knocker as slowly as he could. No sooner had he done it, Draco opened the door, slammed it, and came running towards Harry. He looked worse than Harry had seen him, his hair was messy, and he had dark circles under his eyes. “How did you know we were coming?” Harry enquired. “My Eagle owl was keeping an eye” Draco said pointing towards a huge bird on top of a tree. “Hi Ron, Hi Hermione” Draco said shyly. “Hello, Neville” he extends a hand towards Neville, who after a few seconds of confusion, shook it politely. “Sorry, Hermione and Ron. For being rude to you both and especially Hermione.” Tears began welling in Draco’s eyes. Ron suddenly pulled Draco into a hug, and Hermione gave him a reassuring pat on his shoulder. After Draco consoled himself, he looked a bit more cheerful and a bit better. “So shall we go to McGonagall’s office?”

Chapter-10---

Harry, Ron, Hermione, Neville, and Draco were standing in front of Professor McGonagall, who looked extra stern today. “Where’s Ginny?” she had asked, to which Harry had replied “She was not feeling good” and gave a side glance to Ron, who cleared his throat. “Professor, why did you call us here?” questioned Harry. “First, I want to hear what Neville said about Oswald Godwin Longbottom.” Harry indicated Neville to narrate the myth. “Professor, there were some books and parchments left behind by my great-grandfather. The books were created in such a way that, if any reader holds the book in his hands, it will reflect his future, and words will form on the page by magic. So, Harry held the book in his hands, and all of us were peeking over his shoulder, when something like a prophecy was written on the page. The prophecy was-

When scarred lies fade and truth is clear,

Six shall stand, united here.

Together bound by fate’s own thread,

To seek the Codex long since dead.

Through fractured time and shadowed past,

They’ll find the keys that hold it fast.

But one of fire, born to lead,

Shall claim the crown through word and deed.

No path alone can break the chain,

For only strength in hearts combined

Shall wake the power, forge the key,

And set the hidden spirit free." Said Neville breathlessly.

McGonagall looked thoughtful. She didn't say anything, but her face was scrunched up as if she was thinking. Finally, she addressed Hermione "Do you know what a codex is?" "Yes Professor." Hermione instantly replied. "A codex is a just a fancy word for a book, scroll, or magical document — but in fantasy, it's usually something ancient, secret, and powerful. Also, there was a drawing of the codex. It looked like a gem." "Interesting" said Professor McGonagall pushing her square glasses which matched the markings around her eyes, further up her nose. She paused for a moment or two, and looked a bit anxious, then resumed. "Listen carefully, to what I say. This information should not be shared with anyone else." She took a huge breath and continued "According, to me, this talks about a quest. You need to go on a quest and retrieve keys, which you need to put together and I guess, it reveals the chosen one. But this is not valid information of course. It doesn't make sense and I'm not willing to send you on a fruitless quest." "Professor, please" Draco whined. "This matters. It might reveal who's the chosen one if it's not Harry. We need to find it, as the prophecy had stated 'And when their time comes... the world will never be the same.' We can't take a chance. The CHOSEN ONE might wreak havoc on earth as well. Who knows, he or she, might be worse than..." Draco paused and took a huge breath before saying "Voldemort." Ron's mouth was hanging open. Hermione and Neville looked a bit astonished, McGonagall however, didn't display any emotion... She was deep in thought. "Mr. Malfoy has a point. But I can't risk the life of you all, after whatever you all have gone through." "Please" Hermione pleaded "Professor, the prophecy clearly states six people. Which means Harry, me, Ron, Ginny, Neville, and Draco. After all we're the ones who know about this." "But Hermione, I appreciate your determination, but I can't let you all risk your lives, based on some random prophecy in THE DEPARTMENT OF MYSTERIES." "Professor" Harry thundered "The location was guided to us by, Professor Dumbledore. But do you suspect him?" This seemed to make McGonagall quiet, although she glared at Harry. After long moments of consideration, she said "Alright Potter. I'll give you permission to go on the quest. But you keep me informed of everything." Harry nodded.

“Professor, we have no idea where to start?” complained Ron. “I’ll give you a person’s address. He lives in Hogsmeade. Go and meet him. He has an idea about ‘codex’ and all the advanced branches of magic. He will help you, start your quest. But remember, if you feel there’s any danger, you abandon the quest and return. Clear?” Everyone shook their heads. “Professor, my mother” Ron enquired. “Not a problem Mr. Weasley. I will inform her.” Professor McGonagall waved her wand, and a quill began writing words on a parchment, which she folded it up and gave it to Hermione. “Keep me updated, Potter” she said as we left towards Hogsmeade.

Chapter-11

"Where's No. 3 Thistlewick?" said Draco as we landed in Hogsmeade. "Somewhere to the left of 'Three Broomsticks' said Hermione as she led them there. "Isn't this a shack?" said Ron as we reached there. The roof looked like a patchwork of moss and lichen tiles. The windows looked dull with age and water was dripping down the roof. The roof hung downwards almost kissing the ground. "Let's knock" said Harry as Ron rolled his eyes. Harry knocked on the door and two-three tiles fell from the roof. The tin door creaked, as the owner of the house opened the door. He looked so old, his skin was sagging with wrinkles, and he was a hunch-back. But his eyes shone with knowledge and wisdom. "Welcome" the man stated. Surprisingly, his voice was soft and gentle for his age. He beckoned everyone inside his house, which looked much worse inside. The walls were damp with moss, and the paint was peeling from the walls. There was a painting of a fruit basket, which was the only one that stood intact. Rats were nibbling away the pieces of cloth and all five of them could barely fit in the house. "I think, McGonagall sent you to me, to enquire about the 'Codex.' Am I right? The old man stated. "Sir, we wanted to know how to begin the quest for the Codex." Hermione politely said. "The quest for the Codex, is not an easy one. It requires loyalty, truth, and sacrifice. The three trials are based on these qualities. At last, the chosen one will emerge, but what matters is that you must reach the end of the quest. Are you willing to evaluate these qualities to the maximum potential?" the old man came to an end of his warning. "Sir, we are more than willing to participate in the quest. Am I right, Harry?" Neville questioned. Harry nodded. "Great." The old man went and stood in front of the painting. "There will be a riddle, which you must solve to gain the location for beginning your quest, but you must complete each trial, and you will be shifted to the next trial by magic. Remember, you have to find a 'GEM' in each scenario. Only if you find it, will you be able to go to the next trial. At the end, you have to make a sacrifice. Then, only will the prophecy shed its secrets." Just then came the weird, raspy knock on the tin door. Ron, who was closer to the door, went and opened it to reveal a girl with red hair, brown eyes, and freckles. "Ron" Ginny said as she embraced him. "Woah," Ron said stumbling back. "What's with the sudden affection? And where have you been?" "I went out wandering and then when I came home, Mum said you had gone to meet McGonagall, so I went there, but by that time you left for Hogsmeade and I followed you, till I reached here." Harry could find something strange in her behavior and facial features. Her hair looked a bit dull, and she looked forlorn. She nodded towards Harry and stood beside Draco, who couldn't stop looking at her, as if trying to find something. They were all distracted when the old man muttered a series of spells in Latin- Iusiurando antiquo et lumine occulto, Arcanorum baiulus, ritum revela. Dignis loquere, nemini nega, Ut via ad Codicem obtemperet. There came showers of blue light from the painting, as it thundered and shifted neatly to one side. The whole house rumbled due to the shaking of the painting. Behind the painting, there was a small shelf exquisitely carved in the stone, and on top of the shelf was a folded piece of paper. It was frayed at the edges and pale brown in color. The old man gently picked up the paper, touched it to his head as a sign of pure devotion and handed it over to Draco, who opened it and read it-

" Beneath the gaze of the twin moons bright,
Where Hogwarts' walls hide from sight,
A door awaits with no handle or key,
Whisper the charm forgotten by time,
And the path shall open, as if by rhyme."

"What does it mean?" Harry asked Hermione as they quickly muttered 'Thank you' to the old man and left his house. "I am not sure, Harry. I need time to figure it out." "Why are there so many riddles?" Ron complained. Hermione scowled at him. "One thing is clear from this" Ginny said. "What?" Harry asked her. "It is about some secret chamber in

Hogwarts." "Ginny's right" Hermione beamed at her. "The Chamber is situated inside Hogwarts. Draco, can I have the riddle?" Draco nodded and handed the paper to her. She opened it and scrutinized it for some time. After several minutes, she said "Twin moons bright. It refers to either two windows or two towers. And there is some incantation which has to be said, to open the path." "But there are so many twin windows and towers in Hogwarts. We can't go searching each one. Also, we don't know the incantation" Ron whined. "Ron, you are wrong. There is only one pair of twin windows. It is on the way to the Herbology classroom." Neville looked at Ron. "Great. That is sorted out. But what about the charm or spell?" Harry asked Hermione. "All of you, go where Neville is saying. I'll go to the library and meet you there." Hermione folded the paper and placed it in the front zip of her bag. "Okay, we will meet you there" Neville said as Hermione apparated in front of them. The rest of them made their way towards the Greenhouse. They crossed the Shrieking Shack, Honeydukes and The Three Broomsticks on their way. They walked along the main path leading to the castle gates while admiring the grounds with trees, gardens, and magical creatures. They walked past the courtyard and followed the familiar path towards the greenhouses. “Neville, where is this window?” Draco was exhausted. “Just over here. It should be visible by now. Ah! There it is!” Neville pointed towards a window on the ground floor of the castle. It was misty from outside, otherwise completely normal for an entrance to the Codex. Hermione suddenly apparated behind Ron. “Blimey, Hermione! You scared me!” “Sorry Ron. I found the charm!” “Great. Let’s do it” Harry commented. “Who is going to do it?” All eyes turned towards Hermione. “Me? Fine. Am I supposed to touch it or what?” “I really don’t know. But you can try” Ginny supported her. Hermione took a huge breath and placed her palm on the window. It felt cold to her. “Revelio Arcanum” she murmured gently. Ron was helplessly staring at her, suddenly he caught Harry’s eyes and winked. The window rumbled and shifted to one side, revealing blue swirls behind it. It was almost aquamarine, a delightful, remarkable sight. Harry gestured them to follow him. One by one, they went, accepting their fate and moving on to claim it.

Chapter-12----

As soon as they opened their eyes, they saw Hogwarts before them, but not as they had seen a few minutes before. This Hogwarts was black. The skies overhead had dark clouds preventing the sunlight from penetrating through them and brightening the land. They saw students wearing the school robes with their heads down and no signs of life visible on their faces. All six of them hid behind a bush as they heard footsteps approaching. They eavesdropped on the people. "The Dark Lord has been most merciful to us, John." "Absolutely Arthur. In fact, he proved his supreme power by making Harry Potter- the one who lost in the battle, the headmaster of this pathetic school. And do you know, Lucius Malfoy's son has replaced Severus Snape as the Deputy Headmaster of Hogwarts. What a proud moment, for the Malfoys indeed." "Did they catch that wretched rebel- the Weasley's youngest daughter. What a shame! That they couldn't be of service to the Dark Lord being pure-bloods," said John. "We better get going towards Hogsmeade. Dolohov will be awaiting us." Saying so, they went towards Hogsmeade. "Bloody Hell Harry! You lost the war! That means You-Know-Who controlled your mind and made you Headmaster! And Draco you're the Deputy Headmaster seriously!" Ron exclaimed. "Ron. Keep your voice down." Hermione shushed him. "We better get going, Harry" Ginny said, "If we want to make it to Hogwarts." "Are you mad?" yelled Draco "Can't you see that the place is swarming with death eaters. If anyone of them, sees Harry, we'll be dead." "Draco's right" said Harry "Let's wait." Ginny sighed. After a few minutes later, when the coast was clear, they sneaked inside Hogwarts and hid under the Grand staircase. "Why're we hiding here?" Ginny grumbled. "We should have hidden behind the House points Hourglasses." "Ginny, you want six people to hide behind those hourglasses?!" Ron lost his patience. "Are you mad?" "Shut up, Ron!" Harry thundered. "We need to retrieve the Codex. But how will we search Hogwarts?" "Maybe we can rule out the choices. The Codex is definitely not going to be hidden in classrooms and in the corridors, where people can identify it easily" suggested Hermione. "But what if, it is in the Chamber of Secrets?" stated Neville in a meek voice. "Yes, that is possible, isn't it Harry?" questioned Draco. Harry nodded. "But there is a huge chance of it, being in the trophy room. After all, Codex is a gem" offered Ginny. Harry was in a dilemma; he could go to the Chamber of Secrets as well as The Trophy room. But he had to choose very carefully, for if the death eaters saw him, they would be killed on the spot. Everyone's eyes were on him. He was in the midst of pondering when a new thought made its way into his brain. Ginny had suggested the Trophy Room, so wouldn't it be right? Ultimately, he wanted to impress Ginny, so why not go to the Trophy Room? “Ginny’s right. Let’s go towards the Trophy Room.” Ginny beamed at him. Neville looked a bit disappointed and Draco patted Neville on his shoulder. “Before, we leave. Everyone silence your shoes” Hermione commanded. Everyone nodded and muttered ‘Silencio’ to muffle their footsteps. They crouched in the shadows and came out of hiding. Harry led the way as they used the tapestry of trolls as their cover. Behind it, was a concealed shortcut, which Fred and George had taught Harry. His eyes began to sting with tears. “Harry. Move! There’s someone coming this way!” urged Hermione as Harry entered the shortcut and climbed the first stair and Hermione pushed him forward. He went to the top, stumbling over the steps as Draco came panting at the last. “Did anyone see you?” “No, but it’s advisable to keep going.” They continued their climb and reached the opening of the staircase which led to the suits of armor. Just as Harry, was about to slip past the suit of armor, a death eater came out of nowhere. “Oi! What are you doing here?!” Harry was so startled, that he turned. The Death Eater was astonished. “Harry Potter, the Headmaster, trying to sneak out somewhere!” The Death Eater raised his wand at pointed it towards Harry, at the same time Harry muttered “Stupefy.” The man flew and hit the wall and collapsed on the ground. “Obliviate!”

murmured Hermione behind him. “Let’s go” said Harry as he continued to lead the way towards The Trophy Room. They took a few turns and found themselves facing it. Tucked along the stretch of the corridor, the entrance to the Trophy Room glowed faintly in the sunlight. A pair of oak doors, worn but proud, stood firmly, barricading the entrance to the room. At the top of the door, engraved was the symbol of Hogwarts and the motto ‘Draco Dormiens Nunquam Titillandu’ though moss was creeping along the edges. Harry slowly pushed open the doors of The Trophy Room and beckoned them inside. Initially, it took time to adjust to the darkness, but when their vision was clear, the room looked the same as before. Dust lining the glass boxes in which trophies were kept safely, the walls had numerous cracks and somewhere there was the sound of water dripping. Neville, awed by the glimmering and shining trophies, extended his hand to touch one, when many people apparated in front of them, wearing black robes and silver marks, making the air quiver like a curse. All six of them stood beside Harry, ready with their wands raised. “Well, look who it is" said a remarkably familiar voice, which belonged to Amycus Carrow. “The headmaster himself and the Deputy Headmaster along with all his friends. So, the Dark Lord didn’t fully succeed in defeating you. But he’ll be pleased when I produce your dead body.

Chapter-13----

Alecto raised his wand towards Harry. “Avada Kedavra!” The jet of green light erupted from the tip of his wand. Luckily, everyone dodged it and hid behind the glass cases. “Everyone, wands ready!” yelled Harry.

“Stupefy!”
“EXPELLIARMUS!”

“AVADA KEDAVRA!”

“Reducto!”

“CRUCIO!”

“PROTEGO!”

“Pertrificus Totalus!”

“SECTUMSEMPRA!”

Finally, only Alecto was lying on the floor. “Obliviate” murmured Draco as the memory of their attack, erased from their minds. “Is anyone hurt?” asked Hermione anxiously. “Well, everyone is hurt one way or other” grumbled Neville. Each and every one of them had either a bruise or a minor scratch. “Where’s Ron?!” Hermione yelled, her eyes frantically scanning the entire room. A slight wince came from behind the shelves. Hermione wandered there, saw the sight before him, and knelt down crying. Draco quickly rushed to her aid and saw Ron lying down feebly. Harry, Neville, and Ginny too ran and stood beside Draco. There were deep gashes on his body, bleeding severely and pooling on the floor. He was taking deep breaths and closing his eyes slowly. “No, no, no!” Hermione yelled, causing the glass boxes to quiver. “Ron! Look at me! Nothing’s going to happen to you. You will be fine; I’ll just find a counter curse to this” she muttered desperately. “Harry, when you accidentally used this curse on Draco, did Snape mutter any incantation?” “No, Hermione, I-I don’t know.” Hermione let out a frustrated scream. “Hermione” Ron murmured, his voice breathy. Hermione bent closer to listen to him, tears streaming down her face. “D-d-don’t blame yourself. Il-l-l always be with you” he cupped her cheek in his hands. Hermione looked helplessly, towards Draco. “Draco, please.” Draco was almost on the verge of tears, but he regained his composure and thought calmly for a few seconds. Ron moaned on the floor. Hermione began sobbing uncontrollably. Harry placed his hand on her shoulder to steady her. Draco pointed his wand, towards Ron and murmured “Vulnera Sanentur.” The wounds on Ron’s body began to disappear as if by magic. The wounds were healing and the blood ceased to pour. The color went back to Ron’s face. He looked better as he had healed completely. Except, the scars were still visible. Ron pulled Hermione into a hug, and she broke down. “It's alright, Hermione. I’m fine. How could I go anywhere, without you screaming at me. Hermione smiled. Ron wiped her tears and helped her stand up. He then embraced Harry, Neville and gave a huge pat to Draco. “Thank you, Draco” he murmured and went to hug Ginny. She embraced him but did not cry. Maybe she was strong and her brave mindset, which prevented her from crying after what happened to her brother. “Where, next Harry?” Neville piped up. “Let’s go to the Chamber of Secrets now.” Harry stated.

Chapter-14----

They exited the room after searching it thoroughly. There, they hid behind the shields of armor and towards the stairs, they turned left which led to the staircase to the second floor. They muffled their footsteps and began climbing the stairs. “Ouch, Harry. You stepped on my foot!” complained Ginny. “Sorry” Harry whined. “Hermione” Ron began “When I was about to...” He took a few seconds, deciding which word to use, then came up with an idea. “When I was about to pass out. Wh-why did you look so worried?” he asked timidly. Hermione stopped in her footsteps and turned to look at Ron. He wasn’t looking at her eyes. He was afraid of what might be awaiting for him. He might’ve misread the signs, of her liking him, which could end up in breaking their friendship forever. Hermione didn’t know what to say. This was the first time Ron had shut her mouth. “W-w-w-well because we couldn’t leave you like that. If anything happened to you, your mom would have had a serious shock” she said in her normal voice, concealing whatever she felt for him. She didn’t know exactly what Ron was trying to say. Maybe he would accuse her of liking him while he didn’t. “We’re here” grumbled Draco “Moaning Myrtle’s toilet. How I loathe her.” Suddenly, sounds of footsteps began echoing in the corridor, Draco pushed everyone inside and jumped in. “Ouch, Draco! You gave me a scratch.” “Sorry, Hermione.

But people were coming, and I had to push you all" apologized Draco. "Hermione, are you alright? Draco don't you have sense?!" Ron thundered and went over to Hermione. She just looked at him with wide eyes. All of a sudden, a hysterical laughter came from a cubicle. A ghost of a teenage girl, with a miserable face and round glasses emerged from the cubicle. "Oh, no Harry!" Ginny muttered. "Not her, again!" "Hi, Harry!" Myrtle screamed in her wailing voice. "I haven't seen you since, well- I don't know how many years later I am seeing you. And Draco, hope you're fine!" Draco rolled his eyes. "Harry, open the chamber of secrets. I can't bear her!" whined Ginny. "Me neither. But is everyone willing to come? I mean, it's not a good place to be." Harry questioned. "We're all coming," said Neville. Harry stood in front of the sink, with the tiny snake engraved on top. He focuses, loses his tongue a bit and speaks Parseltogue. The entire sink descends, and a large stone pipe is revealed, the only way to go down. This time, Ginny insists on going first as she can't bear Myrtle. She goes first followed by Harry, Ron, Hermione, Neville, and Draco. The pipe was slimy, cold, and greasy almost like a rollercoaster. They reached the end of the pipe and toppled over each other onto the hard and damp floor. "Oww, Neville! You're on top of me! Ron grumbled. "Sorry Ron" as Neville rolled aside. "We're here guys. The most gross place in

Hogwarts" Ginny said with a disgusted face. They walked through the passage and reached the door to the Chamber of Secrets. The wall is made of stone and snakes are entwined with emeralds glistening in their eyes. Harry hissed in Parseltongue. The door rumbled and opened. They all followed after Ginny, who was sick, on coming to the chamber. "Split up and search, everyone" commanded Ron. They all split up and went in various directions. Suddenly, Neville came running shouting "It's here! It's here!" "Who's here?!" Harry yelled as they all reunited in the center of the chamber. "I-I-I-I don't know" Neville started panicking and shivering. "It looked something like a half spirit and half beast. Look, here it comes, Harry!!!" Neville screamed, pointing towards a creature. It was 8 foot tall, with a wolf-like body and obsidian fur. Its eyes were silver and antlers protruding from its head. Its teeth were sharp, able to tear through flesh and looked almost like the Basilisk; Harry had killed in his second year. Hermione and Ginny screamed. Neville hid behind Draco. Ron was cowering at the last. Harry raised his wand, prepared to defend himself and his friends. The creature came running towards them, with its claws outstretched. Harry thought that moment would be his last as he closed his eyes. He would die as the counterfeit CHOSEN ONE...

Chapter-15----

The beast stopped a few steps in front of Harry. It bowed graciously. Harry looked shocked as the beast started to speak, "My name is Lionel. I haven't come to do any harm." "Then, go away!" Ron stuttered from behind. Lionel growled. "I am here, to assess your loyalty for the Codex." "How do you know, we're here for the Codex?" Hermione whimpered. "I know. The energy which you have gained on passing through the portal is visible to animals. It's different from normal human energy. I can even tell you where the Codex is hidden. But you need to pass my test. Are you willing?" Lionel asked. "Yes, we are," said Harry "And we'll stand together, no matter what." The beast smiled. With a snap of his fingers, he created an illusion of a six-headed dog in front of them and a big, wooden door behind them. "I only have one rule- Listen to what I say." Lionel stated. With another snap of his fingers, he erased their memory temporarily and made them appear dizzy. The six-headed snake began talking to them one-by-one.

Harry- Leave them. They are not yours. They all are sticking to you for fame. Don't be with them. Listen to me and you will be able to pass through the door alone. Your parents, your godfather, Professor Dumbledore, Lupin, Fred, all who you love are waiting on the other side. You only need to let your friends go.

Ron- You're so pitiable. Always overshadowed by brothers and born into a poor family, when you have the talent to succeed. Even the girl you have feelings for-Hermione despises you. You have been nothing under their company. At home, you're overshadowed by brothers and outside by your friends. Listen to me and go through the door alone. Whatever you have ever wanted, wealth beyond imagination lies there. You just need to go alone.

Hermione- You are so brilliant and clever. But what's the point? Everyone sees you as a misfit. They call you names behind your back. Even the friends who you trust call you names. You are continuously called a Mudblood by the society, even though you are wise and matured for it. Ron fakes his feelings for you. Harry uses you for his work. Behind this door, you will find people who accept you as a Muggle born, who will love you, raise you. You just need to walk towards it.

Draco- The boy who always doted on his father. Used to complain to his father if anything happened. What a shame! Your father doesn't even acknowledge you. In fact, he doesn't care about your opinion as well. He forced you to be a Death Eater and follow The Dark Lord blindly. He used you. For getting prestige among the pureblood community. He abandoned your sister when she was only a year old, for prestige, for pride, for prosperity. He only cared about fame. Not even of your poor mother, lying sick and unwell. Through these doors you will find your happy family. An ideal father, your sister, and your mother as healthy as ever. You only need to walk and leave everyone behind.

Neville- Neville Longbottom, the timid son of Frank and Alice Longbottom, is how people address you. Your life was shattered when Bellatrix tortured your parents to insanity. Your friends, ridicule you as the boy whose parents went mad. Your grandma, strict and stern, has failed to give your mother and father's love. Walk through the doors and you will find your united family. Your mother and father, fine as ever and your grandmother kind and simple. You only need to walk alone.

The six-headed snake persisted everyone. Harry cried "I want my family; I want Professor Dumbledore and everyone else. But I want my friends as well." The snake forced Harry "There's no point staying with your friends. They all would leave you the moment they got what they wanted." "No. I want them. I won't leave them and go. They have been with me since the beginning. I won't leave without them!" Harry yelled. Suddenly a thunderous sound flashed, and Harry was taken back to the Chamber of Secrets. He found himself on the floor. He swiftly got up and interrogated Lionel "Where are my friends? Why are they not here? Why do I feel dizzy? And why is only Ginny here? Harry pointed towards her. "Calm, down Harry" Lionel said in a soothing voice. "I had casted a spell on you, so that you forget everything temporarily, but the spell has lifted as you have passed the loyalty test. You disagreed with meeting your family and your loved ones and chose your friends. If your friends have passed the loyalty test, they will be here soon. As for Ginny, she passed her test quiet earlier." "But I didn't see you, Ginny" Harry asked her. "I was right behind you, Harry. You were too dizzy to turn." Ginny said. No sooner had she said that Draco and Ron came out of nowhere and Draco embraced Harry and started weeping. "Pottah! Th-th-that thing, talked about my sister. I-I-I can't..." "It's alright, Draco." Harry consoled him. Hermione and Neville also came beside them. Hermione was sweating profusely and ran towards Ron, who opened his arms and allowed her to embrace him. "Ron! It said tha-that you didn't like me, and you faked your feelings for me." She was about to cry when Ron lifted her chin up and forced her to meet his gaze. "Listen to me" he murmured, his breath on her cheek. She looked at him. He gently touched his forehead to hers. "Let anybody say anything. Don't listen to them. You are my past, present and future. You're the only one who understood me for who I am, and I'm forever grateful to you. Before I die, on this quest, I just want to say that I love you. I really love you." Hermione was laughing and crying at the same time. "Blimey, you look so cute when you laugh or cry." She smiled. "Will you love me forever?" He nodded and said "I will love you until, the sun rises in the east, until the moon shines brightly in the sky, until the stars sparkle in the night sky, until..." He paused for an example. Then smiled and said, "until you continue fighting with me." She laughed and Ron smiled. She put her hand on his collar and tugged him closer until she could feel his breath ghosting her lips. She pulled him impossibly closer. Mere inches separated them from each other until Harry coughed and they left each other immediately. By that time, Harry had consoled Draco, Neville looked a bit steady, and Ginny looked less exhausted. "Lionel, we all passed the test. Give us the location now." Lionel smiled and said "Well done All! You have proved your loyalty. You went against your own desires and chose your friends. Such friendship is rare. A gem, to be precise. You have passed the first trial. You will find the Codex, in the Room of Requirement. Proud of you." With a double snap of his fingers, he transported all of them, in front of the Room of Requirement.

Chapter-16---

"Wow" that was unexpected said Draco as they stood outside the Room of Requirement nestled along the quiet stretch of the seventh corridor, opposite a large tapestry of Barnabas the Barmy. The wall looks utterly ordinary; only when someone paces past three times, concentrating on the seeker's need, does a door melt into view, carved into the wall. "Harry, someone's coming" hissed Ginny as they heard footsteps and mild chattering of students coming this way. "Everyone, listen. We all know how to use the room, so I'm not explaining in a detailed manner. Concentrate on finding the Codex. Keep telling yourself 'I need to find the hidden Codex.' We can't afford to waste time, as students are heading this way." He spoke quickly and everyone began walking past the wall, concentrating hard on the Codex. "Its not working, Harry!" Neville whined. "Keep trying, Neville!" Harry screeched as the students came even closer. Each and every one of them, closed their eyes and focused deeply on the Codex. The door came into view and Harry immediately pushed open the door, as the students came into view. "Hurry up, everyone!" he yelled and pushed everyone inside and jumped along with them. The door sealed itself, like a normal magic door barricading, everyone from outside, unless summoned with purpose. "Did anyone see us, Harry?" Hermione looked anxious. "I don't think so" Harry replied. They turned their heads towards the direction of the room, and saw what was awaiting them. Cracked stone floors, lay beneath them, wide beneath a towering ceiling. Scorched walls bore the scars of exploded spells, while ruined pillars and rubble offered cover to anyone who entered. Floating torches illuminated the ruins while the air was thick with smoke, the curses cast by warriors. The Room had shifted into a war-ready arena. It was a battlefield, ready for war. "Blimey, Harry! Is-Is-Is that a battlefield?!" Ron whimpered. No sooner had he said this, almost a dozen wizards came from thin air. They looked young, muscular, and scary. The scars lining their bodies, reflected the people who had sacrificed their lives to this room. One of the wizard, in a guttural voice spoke "You have to fight us, to retrieve the Codex. You defeat us, you will get the Codex. You lose; you will be our slave. Draco gulped. Neville and Ron looked like they were about to faint. Hermione's hand was trembling. Harry was nervous. Ginny looked calm and unfazed, the flame of anger burning in her eyes, ready to burn everything in her path. "Are you ready?" the wizard spoke. Harry turned to look at others, for their opinion. They seemed frozen in shock. Harry took the decision himself; he could leave everything right now and go back to the Burrow. But the entire world will be in greater danger if he doesn't find the Chosen One. He nodded. The battle lines were drawn. The wizards raised their wands. Harry took a huge breath; this choice was between life and death. 3.., 2..., 1..., Go! The wizards shot a string of curses at them. "Protego!" yelled Harry as he cast a shield for all of them. "Guys" he said struggling to hold the shield "I need you all to help me. We need to do this. Come on!" Everyone else nodded. Harry signaled to them and left the shield. At that very instant, Hermione, Draco and Ginny shot curses at them, while Ron and Neville defended them. "PETRIFICUS TOTALUS!" Hermione shouted blasting one of the wizards in a full body-bind curse. "STUPEFY!" one of the wizards yelled as Hermione was blasted across the room and crumpled to the ground. "HERMIONE!" Ron cried in agony. "I'LL TAKE REVENGE FOR THIS, YOU GREAT BRUTE! SECTUMSEMPRA!" The wizard who had blasted Hermione, now lay on the ground, screaming with slashes fresh on his body and blood pooling on the ground. "INCENDIO!' one of the wizards thundered. A ball of fire, emerged from the tip of his wand, which he blasted towards Neville. "AGUAMENTI!" Neville shrieked as water from his wand, extinguished the fire. "CONFRINGO!" shouted Ginny as two of the wizards were blasted into pieces. "LOCOMOTOR MOTIS!" Draco yelled as one of the wizards, who was going to cast a spell in his direction, bound his legs tightly together, making him unable to walk or stand as he fell to the ground. "BOMBARDA MAXIMA" screamed the wizard standing behind him. The blast severely impacted Neville and Draco who flew across the room and landed heavily on the round. Ron was on the verge of tears. He and Harry together yelled "PROTEGO MAXIMA!" to shield themselves and Ginny from the spells. Ginny's eyes were red with anger. Her face was swollen, and she was breathing heavily. "ENTRAIL-EXPELLING!" shrieked Ginny, pointing towards two wizards. They tried shielding themselves, but the force of the spell was so huge, it hit them both with great impact. Their entrails such as intestines, guts came sloshing out of their bodies and spread over the ground. Harry startled, looked at Ginny. She was unfazed, concentrating on the remaining wizards left. "I need you both to protect me" she murmured to Harry and Ron as she casted a shield towards a spell headed towards her. Ron looked at Harry and said something, but he couldn't hear because Ginny had uttered "FIENDFYRE!." A huge serpent made of fire came charging towards the wizards. They tried all the protective spells, but they couldn't tame it, as Harry knew very well, due to his experience before the Battle of Hogwarts. The wizards were consumed in the fire. The room was eerily quiet. Then, out of their remains the wizards came alive. Harry and Ron were left gaping. Ginny became ready to duel, if required. The wizards smiled, the one with the guttural voice spoke “I admire your bravery, Ginny. It takes a great deal of courage to cast the spells you have done. I admire resilience and gallantry in the face of death. But you all have performed exceptionally well. You supported your friends and remained calm under pressure. Once again, you have proved your loyalty. These days, it’s not easy to find loyalty. Reliability is something, which is rare, a precious gem these days. You and your friends have passed the first trial successfully. Your reward is the Codex.” The wizard waved his wand and a pedestal carved with wolves and eagles with an engraving that said ‘Fidelitas, gemma illa constans, omnes thesauros virgae magicae vel mago notos superat.’ A velvet cushion rested on the pedestal with a Spessartine garnet shone majestically, reflecting the light falling on it. The wizard gestured for Harry to take it. “Fidelitas, gemma illa constans, omnes thesauros virgae magicae vel mago notos superat” the wizard said ”Meaning- "Loyalty, that constant gem, surpasses all the treasures known to the magic wand or wizard, is bestowed upon you. May you succeed in your quest” as Harry held the gem in his hands. It felt cool and smooth also, it looked like a drop of Molten Lava. “Sir” Ron was crying and on his knees, in front of the wizard “Can you please revive Hermione, along with Neville and Draco.” The wizard nodded and placed a hand on Ron’s shoulder. “Your love for Hermione is unconditional. I am proud of your commitment to her." Waving his wand at their crumbled bodies, Neville and Draco stirred and got up. Hermione, opened her eyes, while Ron was aldready beside her. With her strength, coming back, she was able to stand up. "For a second, I thought, I lost you, Hermione" cried Ron as he embraced her and broke down. "I am fine, Ron. Nothing's happened to me. I am alright."Hermione assured him. He controlled his emotions and saw Ginny and Harry tending to Draco and Neville. "Harry, You found the Codex!" Hermione rejoiced. Harry handed it over to her, and she kept it securely in her bag. Suddenly, the Room of Requirement doors, began shaking. Someone was trying to enter the Room. "Harry what do we do?" asked Neville, trembling. The answer was given by the wizard "Go, through the portal . It will lead you to the second trial. Go, Now!!" casting a spell from his wand, a portal appeared out of nowhere, its pink and purple swirls inviting. "Go. Now! I cant keep this portal open for a longer time!" Ron was the first one to run across the room, holding Hermione's hand with Ginny at his heels. Neville and Draco also followed him, while Harry was the last. The door of the Room, threatened to open with each passing second. Ron and Hermione went through the portal, so did Ginny and after her followed Neville, Draco. Harry was about to pass, when the door burst open and entered Harry. But a more darker and evil version than him. He looked like a death eater, with overgrown hair and an evil smile, the dark mark burnt on his skin. Also, he did not have the lightning-scar on his forehead. The Headmaster of Hogwarts was astonished to see himself, standing in front of him. Draco held Harry's hand and pulled him through the portal, just as the killing curse whizzed over their heads.

Chapter-17----------

Draco fell on top of Harry as they landed onto the ground below. But, the ground wasn't made of soil or stone. It shimmered lightly, as if made woven with ancient spells, like glass but not fragile. "Where are we?" Harry mumured as Draco moved aside, giving him space to get up. He looked around. The surroundings shimmered in air, like a magical realm to protect bystanders. There where shards of glass lying on the ground and rubble lying in a pile. Power was floating through air, with blue, red sparks like magic. The sky was covered with dark clouds, hanging low, making it difficult to see anything. "Lumos" murmured Ron and everyone did the same. Hermione answered "I dont know. But this place looks a bit old. I also know, that we're not supposed to be here." "How do you know that?" Ron enquired. She rolled her eyes at him. "Because the surroundings are glimmering, like a magical arena." They were shouts coming from a few feet away. "I think, we should stay here." Ginny said. "No" stated Neville "We won't know what is going on, if we keep staying here." "Both of you have a point" Draco sighed. "If we stay here, we will be safe but we also won't know what is going on. I think we should, wait here for a few minutes and then go." Harry nodded in agreement. All six of them sat together, eavesdropping on the shouts coming a few feet away. "Ginny, I wanted to ask you something."

Ron said. "What is it?" "How the hell did you even know th-th-the spell, in which you know" he made a prodding movement with his hands. "That. I had seen it in the library, when we were learning spells for Dumbledore's Army" she tossed her hair behind. "But how could..." Harry interrupted him. "Sshh Ron! I think we should go now, its really dark and I don't fancy the idea of staying here alone." "How on earth will the Codex be here?" complained Draco. "Dont know" Hermione replied. They walked a few feet unless, they saw two grown men, arguing in the darkness. They had to squint their eyes to see who it was. Hermione pushed them behind a barrel. "What, Hermione?" Harry lowered his voice. "D-d-dont you see who it is?" Hermione's voice was trembling. Realization and shock was coating her face. On seeing the confusion,in everyone's face, she said "IT'S DUMBLEDORE AND GRINDELWALD!!" Ron, Draco, Neville and Ginny were left gaping. Harry didn't quite understand. "I don't understand, Hermione." She was almost going to cry. "Harry, this is the battle of Dumbledore and Grindelwald in 1945! Both were the greatest wizards of all time, but Grindelwald became evil and Dumbledore decided to fight him. They were childhood friends as well. No-no-no! The Codex, cant be here. Its a mistake!!" A flash of light appeared before them and out of the light, emerged Lionel. "Lionel! Hermione yelled. "This is a mistake! The

Codex can't be here. Its bizarre!" "Hermione" Lionel spoke in his soft voice "The Codex is here. You have time travelled to the distorted memory of the battle where Dumbledore defeated Grindelwald in 1945. But someone altered it and Grindelwald will win. You must regain the trust of Dumbledore and fight alongside him. The Codex is locked in Grindelwald's wand. Also, you must suceed in defeating Grindelwald otherwise the future will be altered forever. That is all I can tell you. The rest will be revealed by Dumbledore himself." Saying so, Lionel vanished leaving the air, thick with smoke behind him. "Pottah, we have to speak to Dumbledore" argued Draco. No way! He won't recognize us!" Neville shrieked. "Well, someone has to do it. Is anyone, willing to try?" Everyone shook their heads. "Great" Harry muttered as he clutched his wand tightly, and paced slowly towards Dumbledore. He was still arguing verbally, with Grindelwald. Lucky, thought Harry. If they had started the duel, he could never even talk to Dumbledore, leave retriving the Codex. He was right behind Dumbledore, when he cleared his throat and said "Professor Dumbledore, Sir" Dumbledore turned to look at him; a bit surprised. "Who are you?" he asked in a stern voice. "I'm Harry, sir. Harry Potter, from the future. I have been sent to fight the battle alongside you." "How can I trust you, Mr. Potter?" Harry's heart shook. "You have to trust me please. It's been foretold that

Grindelwald will win the war." Dumbledore suddenly pointed his wand to his neck "Whose spy are you?!" "Sir, I am no one's spy" Harry whimpered "Please trust me!" "Fine. I will, trust you. One one condition. You have to complete the trial set by me. Are you ready?" Harry nodded. "Very well then." Dumbledore waved his wand and and a magical challenge, appeared in front of them. "This challenge, is called 'The Flame of Fides'. Pass the challenge, and you shall regain my trust. If you fail, I will consider you as a spy and.." Dumbledore paused. Harry gulped. Dumbledore disappeared. Harry entered the maze. It was like the same one, from the Triwizard Tournament, but a little bit smaller. He raised his wand and mumured "Lumos" as he walked deeper inside the maze. When, he turned right, he suddenly saw an illusion of Dumbledore looking at him. The illusion began to speak in a distorted voice. "You must speak the forgotten truth. If you are indeed from the future, and close to Dumbledore, then you must share a truth about Dumbledore which only he himself would know. But, if it causes Dumbledore pain, you will be forced into your most painful memory. You have three chances." Harry was in a fix. If this was Hermione, she would have answered all questions correctly. He was not good with riddles. Harry closed his eyes and concentrate, the first thing which came to his mind was Ariana Dumbledore- his sister. Harry raised his chest and spoke in a stable voice - You were the one who wanted to wait. Aberforth begged you not to chase dreams with Gellert. And when Ariana died, it was *your silence* that kept the guilt buried... not just yours — but Aberforth's too. He never forgave you. Not really. Not even when he watched you die." At that moment, Harry's chest burns as though he's shouldering the weight of sorrow, grief, and regret. He bends on his knees, began clutching his chest with both hands, his wand forgotten on the floor. Harry wheezed "I said the answer. W-why is this happening?" "This is causing Dumbledore guilt and regret. His pain never healed. You have two more chances." The burden on Harry's chest lifted. He was able to stand up, clutching his wand firmly. He again closed his eyes and concentrated firmly; on every single word Dumbledore had spoken about himself. He scanned through his recollections. He desired a Pensieve. Something not related to the death of Arianna, something.... A truth clicked in his mind. He looked at the illusion-Dumbledore and said – "You asked to be buried with your wand. But that is not the actual reason, you wanted to stay away from Arianna, by being buried far from her. Because you didn't believe, you deserved to rest beside her." A pain greater than the previous one, a wave of cold dreariness and loneliness, coursed through his body like standing before a grave. His own emotions hit him in the chest- the fear of losing his parents,

Sirius, Fred, Lupin all of them. Harry, screamed in agony. “Please” he whispered. “Please, stop this.” The Illusion-Dumbledore snapped his fingers, and he found himself breathing fresh, cold air again. Free of all the guilt and sorrow. “One last chance” Dumbledore said. Harry was going mad. He had said all he knew. Something not related to Arianna, something not related to her death. Was it related to the Elder wand? To power? Yes, to power. At that moment, the last piece of the puzzle clicked in Harry’s mind. “You once said it was your greatest regret — not Ariana’s death, but that you waited too long to do the right thing. That power scared you because you tasted it once, and you liked it. And you let it cost you everything.” The Illusion-Dumbledore flinched. The air around them thickened with fog. Harry awaited the sharp pain. But nothing happened. The Illusion-Dumbledore cracks into pieces. A voice says “Well Done, Harry. You have proved that you know Dumbledore. Keep walking, you will be facing the second challenge.” Harry collected his wand from the ground, and walked a bit further, not believing his luck. He had done a random guessing. He felt confident about the next challenge. He walked a few steps and saw The Mirror of Erised facing him. The same gold frame and clawed feet along with the inscription ‘Erised stra ehru oyt ube cafru oyt on wohsi.’ The young Dumbledore came through the maze and stood in front of Harry.

"Walk towards the mirror, Harry" Dumbledore said calmly. Harry walked towards the mirror and was taken aback by what he saw. He saw corrupted versions of himself- betraying Dumbledore, power-hungry versions of himself- allying with Voldemort, broken versions of himself- kneeling and crying in front of the graves of his parents, Sirius, Lupin, Fred, Dobby, Dumbledore. These feelings began to plague Harry in real life. The feelings of guilt, regret, betrayal, pain, sorrow, power began to swirl in his head. He clutched his head and collapsed on the ground, writhing and screaming, asking the voices in his head to go away. It seemed as though, the mirror spoke to him. "I will name five qualities. You need to tell me your deepest secrets and desires based on these secrets. But only speak the truth. For if you lie, you will be trapped inside this maze forever." The pain in Harry's head increased ten times. He was screaming and yelling in pain. The mirror, however, paid no heed. "The five qualities are guilt, resentment, fear, survivor, and willingness. Your trial begins now." Harry thought his skull was going to crack into two pieces. He writhed on the ground. A small voice in his head ordered him to focus, to answer the questions and leave from here. Harry complied with it. He yelled "For the first quality- guilt. I carried the cup, and bought him there, to his death. I can't undo that, but I wish I could. I was the one who was supposed to die, instead of him. But he... died" Harry began weeping in pain. "Resentment- I resented Dumbledore, for not telling me any of his secrets and leaving me in the dark. Till the end. But now I realize, it was for my safety." The pain in his head was threatening to kill him, with each passing second. "I'll tell you!" Harry screeched "I was afraid of becoming the enemy. Unable to think of hurting everyone who cared for me. I was afraid of Voldemort controlling me, I didn't want to think about it. For survivor- I wish I never survived. I wish Voldemort had killed me, along with my parents. I would be with them. I would never be the Chosen one. Never had to see Sirius, Dobby, Fred, and everyone else die in front of me." His scar hurt more than ever. Harry clutched it tightly and was rolling here and there. He couldn't think of willingness. What was he willing to do? What was it? He finally uttered the secret he had preserved for long. "If I must die. I am willing to. I am willing to walk into death's arms, embrace him like an old friend and not look back." The pain in his head slowly subsided. He lay panting on the ground. Dumbledore gently walked up to him and waved his wand. The pain gradually disappeared. Harry was able to stand up. "One last challenge, is waiting for you, Harry." He said as he disappeared.

Chapter-18-----

Harry got to his feet and began wandering. It seemed that he had been walking for several minutes, he eventually grew tired. His feet were aching, and his head was still fuzzy. Finally, he saw something in front of him, a pedestal on which two identical wands were placed, and an egg was floating on top of them. His eyes darted on the instructions engraved on the side. He gently rubbed the dust on top of it and read it "Two identical wands are presented- one leads to manipulation and the other one to truth. You must choose based on what feels right, not based on power. If you are wrong, the phoenix egg will vanish but if you are right, it will hatch mid-air. You have to choose the phoenix's path." Does he have to find out what the wand is made up of? He has no idea. He is not Ollivander- the maker of wands. His brain was still fuzzy. Harry couldn't come to a decision, so he hovered his hand directly over each of the wand and instantly pulled back. He could feel a vibration, an essence of some sort in the air. Harry, with uncertainty, gently touched the first wand, it lets out a low growl which echoes through the mist. He moved towards the second wand and placed his fingers gently on top of it, this wand lets out a soft cry, almost like the call of a phoenix chick. Understanding, coats Harry's face. A growl and a call of a phoenix chick. These must be the cores- The core of the first wand is Dragon Heartstring, and the core of the second wand is Phoenix Feather. He had deciphered the cores. Now what, could be the wood? The mist grew, making it harder to see anything. "Lumos" Harry muttered, the tip of his wand ignited. He held his own wand, over the ones lying on the pedestal. The one with the Dragon Heartstring core looked almost black, with a smooth grain that catches little light. He could feel a sense of power and control coursing through him. The wand made him feel as if he could conquer the world. Harry immediately kept the wand and lifted the other wand. The Phoenix Core wand looked pale, almost ivory and gleamed in the light from his wand. This time, he could feel hope and renewal. All those who died, have a chance of coming back alive. He could feel it. It also seemed to connect to his heart, sending sparks through his veins. He gently left it and pulled back. Everything seemed to fit perfectly. The one with the Dragon Heartstring was made of Ebony. And the one with the Phoenix Feather is his wand, made of Holly. He immediately knew what he had to choose. His hand hovered over the wand made of Holly, the phoenix egg shook. Knowing this was the right choice, he picked it up and said aloud "This is the wand." The phoenix egg shook violently. Harry went a few steps back. The egg burst open and instead of a phoenix-chick, Dumbledore emerged out of the egg and stood beside him. A golden-yellow trail came floating from nowhere and created a memory. Dumbledore saw his future, older version, smiling and placing a hand on Harry. "If I am to trust you as, the man I become, then I will trust you now." Harry smiled and nodded. Dumbledore held his hand, and they apparated, from where Harry had left for the trials. The ground was filled with fissures, and the walls had huge cracks and dents in them. The pile of rubble was now spread all over the ground. Ron, Hermione, Draco, Neville, and Ginny were standing and watching something in the distance. They all were hurt, either in the form of bruises or scratches. Harry ran to them, and Ginny embraced him. He flushed, while Ron looked away and smiled. "What happened?" Harry asked. With a trembling finger, Draco pointed in the distance. At first, Harry couldn't see anything. Then his eyes gradually adjusted to the darkness, he saw the figure of Grindelwald bent on his knees, on the ground. The Elder Wand lay forgotten on the ground, as Harry ran to pick it up, Dumbledore placed a hand on his shoulder and indicated him to wait; while he himself went ahead and picked up the wand, twirled it in his hands and handed it to Harry. As soon as Harry touched the wand, it began to throb and pulse in his hands. He dropped the Wand on the ground. The Wand began to pound on the ground. "Harry, do not drop the Wand" Dumbledore said as Harry picked it up swiftly. The wand continued to pulse in his hand. His heartbeat matched the throbbing of the wand. The wand flew mid-air. "Noooo! That is my wand!!!!" Grindelwald screeched. With a wave of his wand, Dumbledore muttered "Incarcerous," Grindelwald was bound by invisible ropes. The wand, floating in air, with a sudden crack, exploded and the pieces rained down. Out of the wand, the Codex emerged, an Aquamarine pale-light blue. It floated in the air and gently landed in the hands of Hermione, who held it and kept it safely in her bag. Dumbledore smiled and said "You all have completed the second trial and retrieved the Codex from Grindelwald's wand. You have proven the value of truth, honesty, and trust. Trust is not easy to gain. The need of a human mind to believe someone is really too much. To gain someone's trust, there are a lot of sacrifices and promises to make. You all have performed efficiently. I am proud of you all." With a swirl of his wand, he created a portal, this time with red and orange swirls. "See you in the future, Harry." Dumbledore smiles as everyone passed the portal. Harry felt a drop of tear, falling from his eyes.

Chapter -19---

The portal led them to Hogwarts again. But not the one controlled by the death eaters; the same old Hogwarts, in which they grew, which taught them the values of friendship, of strength, how to face battles etc. The place where they grew from their childhood into adulthood. They landed on the soft grass gently. Harry noticed Ron's leg having a huge stitch but set aside his worry. "What happened to you guys, when I was facing the challenge?" Harry immediately questioned them. "Nothing, Harry." Hermione looked skeptical. Harry eyeing their bruises, scratches, raised an eyebrow. "Well, actually Harry, we were fighting Grindelwald" stated Draco coolly. Hermione punched him on the face. "What was that for?" he whined. "Hermione. Relax" Ron said, pulling her towards him. "As Draco said, Dumbledore wanted us to keep Grindelwald busy, until you came out of the challenge. That's why we're all covered in bruises" concluded Ginny. "What's your problem Hermione? Why don't you want me to know?" Harry screamed at her. "Harry, chill. Please. Hermione's in a bit of shock" begged Ron. Hermione began crying. Ron consoled her and glared at Harry. "Grindelwald used a 'Ossis Frango' curse on Ron" sighed

Ginny. “What spell is that?!” Harry thundered beginning to lose his patience. “Even we didn’t know, Harry” muttered Ron “He targeted the bone in my leg and snapped it” Hermione began weeping uncontrollably. “It must be some dark magic, luckily Ginny knew the correct counter-curse.” “Hermione, tried everything. But it wouldn’t work. She was devastated and thought that Ron would……” paused Draco. “Its alright, Hermione. I’m completely fine.” Ron lifted her chin up to meet his eyes. His eyes softened on seeing her. “You will never get rid of me that easily.” Ron smiled, Hermione giggled and shoved him playfully. “Harry, how was your trial?” Neville interrupted. Harry told them all about his challenge. Starting from trying to gain Dumbledore’s trust to facing the challenges, how did he manage to survive it all and the bear brutality of it? Everyone listened intently. When Harry concluded, Ginny swung her arms around his shoulder and pulled him into a hug. Harry stumbled over while Ron cleared his throat. “We better get going,” said Draco. “Is this our normal Hogwarts?” Ron enquired. “What do you mean by normal Hogwarts?” Neville rolled his eyes. “Well, the one without any death eaters.” “Of course, it is” said Ginny “Can’t you see, Ron?”

Ron looked sheepish. "Come on, guys. Let's go" urged Harry. "But, where do we go, inside the castle?" asked Hermione. "I don't know. Should we go to the Room of Requirement or the Chamber of Secrets again?" Ginny looked doubtful "I don't think so. Let us enter the castle fast" Neville was curious. Harry led everyone from behind the bush towards Hogwarts. It looked so familiar, so intriguing. Harry would never forget the first time he entered through those doors. The castle rose out of the fading mist; its towers etched against the evening sky like an old friend waiting patiently for him to return. Harry drew in a sharp breath, forcing his eyes to the castle's familiar silhouette. This was his Hogwarts, scarred but unbroken. The one worth fighting for. But as he stepped forward, the truth settled heavy in his heart — Hogwarts would always be his home, and his burden. Harry pushed open the great doors and stepped inside. The hall was eerily quiet and silent. It looked as if many hushed secrets were floating in the air noiselessly. The echo of their feet stomping on the gravel could be heard. "Why is it so quite?" Neville voiced out the common question. "I honestly don't know" Harry's voice echoed throughout the castle. "I think the castle is an illusion" Hermione was skeptical. "But illusions aren't real and involve physical interaction. I can touch this, look" Draco touched the wall. It seemed solid and rigid as ever. "I think, Hermione's right. It can be a tangible illusion. Can't it?" Ginny questioned. "Brilliant, Ginny!" Hermione squealed. "Yes, a tangible illusion, an illusion which looks real and can be interacted with." "Where do we go, now?" Ron began losing his patience. "It usually shows us some clue but now it isn't showing anything" Harry sighed. At that moment, Hermione's bag began to shake violently. It was struggling to break free from her hold and she was trying to hold it in. "Ron! Harry!" she shrieked. Harry and Ron swiftly turned their heads. "My Bag! It is trying to break free! I don't know what to do!" Ron ran and helped her pull the bag, but the bag was too headstrong on leaving her. Ron tugged and toppled on the floor, but the bag did not yield. "Immobulus!" muttered Hermione. But the bag did not stop flying. "Wait Hermione!" Harry yelled "Let the bag go!" "Are you mad?!" Ron screamed. "Both the Codex are inside your bag. Maybe it is just trying to show us the location of the third codex. Just leave it!" Hermione nodded in understanding and left her grip on the bag. It began soaring towards the air, as if someone was summoning it. Everyone ran after it. It hovered for a few moments, near the Great Hall, turned right and shot up. Harry ran up the stairs. It entered the library and flew directly towards the Restricted Section and fell on the ground. “What happened?” panted Draco behind him. “I don’t know. It entered the Restricted Section and dropped on the ground.” “Hermione, what do we do?” Ron asked her. “Maybe, it is asking us to pull a book from the shelf. I want you to pull every book on this shelf. This is where the bag fell.” She lifted the bag and slung it over her shoulders. Everyone began pulling various books from the shelf; It was when Ginny pulled a book titled “Secrets of the Founders,” the shelf rumbled, and she stepped back. Neville and Ron toppled over. The shelf moved aside to reveal a spiral staircase, similar to the one leading to Dumbledore’s office. “Lumos” Harry murmured as he led the way down the staircase. The corridors were dusty; the air thick with invisible voices that were whispering secrets or warning. Ron held Hermione as he went down. Draco clutched Harry’s shirt, while Neville was cowering at the last. Ginny, not being afraid of anything was bravely descending down. “Oof!”

Harry groaned. "What's the matter, Harry?" Ginny uttered behind him. "I think I have found a door. But I cannot find the handle." Harry grappled with the door, fumbling for the handle. "Harry, look" Hermione pointed her wand towards the wand. Something was inscribed on the wall in a strange language. It was more of figures, like hieroglyphics, but couldn't be understood that easily. "Which language is this?" Draco traced the patterns on the wall. "I think I have seen this somewhere before. But I don't remember where?" "This is Eryndal" Ginny said simply. "Ery—what?" Ron was baffled. "Eryndal, Ron. I know this language and I can read it." "How do you know this strange Ery- whatever language?" "I read it in books." "I never knew, you read Ginny?" Hermione was taken aback. "I do read sometimes. But I like to learn things. I was reading a book of strange, undeciphered languages and I learnt this." "Well, what does this say?" Neville piped up. "It says 'Greetings! You must have succeeded on the quest for the two Codex previously. But Beware! For the access to the Third Codex is not an easy task. It requires sacrifice and teamwork. Not a task for the faint-hearted. Be Vigilant! You have been warned!'" "It requires sacrifice?" Ron directed his wand towards Harry's face. "Let us hope, it doesn't emphasize on the value," Draco murmured under his breath. Harry went towards the door. "Harry, Don't do it!" Ron screamed. "We have to sacrifice someone. Let's just go from here!" "Abandon everything and go!" thundered Ginny. "After all the hard work we did, you want us to leave. If the unknown Chosen one rises, the world will be destroyed or won't even exist!" Harry looked at Ron's pleading face and Ginny's bravery. He took a huge breath. The fate of the world rested once again on his shoulders. If he found the Codex, the Chosen one would be revealed. But if he didn't, the Chosen one will remain unknown and uncharted and may destroy the world. "I'm sorry, Ron. Ginny's right." He gulped and pushed open the doors.

Chapter-20-----

It was a tiny circular room with creepers that reached up towards the ceiling. The ceiling was carved with intricate swirls and patterns. The floor was thick with dust, as if no one had ever trodden on this surface. The air was thick with hushed voices and whispers. The room was covered in pillars and curiously, there were holes in each wall. The pillars were carved with roses and wands and words were written in that same language which Ginny had deciphered earlier. In the midst of the room, stood a pedestal, on top of which a fierce flame was floating. It flickered in rage, daring anyone to come closer and touch it. Suspended within the flame, was the last and final Codex. Its vibrant and menacing red shade was the only source of light and fear in the room. It stood magnificently, surpassing all the gems in the world. A fine line was present on the ground separating them from the Codex. A hoarse voice echoed throughout the room. "You all have made it to the final chamber, but do you have what it takes to win the Codex? The hunt for this particular Codex is not an easy task. To redeem the Codex suspended within the fiery flame, you must channel your magic together, to create a protective circle of light, to shield yourself from the heat and brutality of the flame. Only if you do so, will the Codex be yours. Fail to succeed, and the flames will escort you to hell. The choice is yours." "Bloody Hell. What was that all about?!" Ron began to slowly walk towards the pedestal, while the flame became enraged and charged towards him. The flame died as he stumbled behind the line. "Are you alright?" Harry questioned him. "I am fine. Blimey, it almost burned me." "How are we going to channel our magic?" Neville was sweating. "Maybe we can try some spells to extinguish the fire." "Good one Draco" Ginny said. Hermione raised her wand. "Let me go first." She pointed her wand towards the pedestal; and muttered "Aguamenti Maxima." The torrent of water, which was released from her wand, began surging back towards them and drenched them fully. "I am sorry. I thought it would work" she apologized. "Let me try" Harry pointed his wand "Extinguisho." Nothing worked. The flames were raging as ever. "How do we channel our magic? Isn't it about doing magic? And that is what we're doing." Ron whined. "I got it! I got it!" Neville began jumping up and down. "Hold on, Neville! Otherwise, the flames will consume you. What did you understand?" Draco warned. "It is simple! The voice spoke about channeling our magic and in the prophecy from the book in my library, it also spoke about 'strengths in hearts combined.' So, isn't it obvious?!" Hermione slapped her head "Of course. Neville's right. We need to cast spells together which will stop the fire." Neville beamed at her. "Okay everyone, let us try 'Aguamenti Maxima' together. Form a circle." Harry commanded. They did as he said. Behind the line, they formed a circle, with their backs pressed together. "Everyone point your wand in the direction of the flame" Draco stated. With the tips of their wands pointed towards the flame, they looked at each other. "To the count of three" Ginny counted. "One... Two... Three!" "Aguamenti Maxima!" six voices echoed around the room. The torrents of water emerging from their wands headed towards the flame but then backfired and drenched them again. "Why is it not working?!" Harry screamed in frustration. Ron went to console him. "Harry. Calm down. We will work something out. Please, stay calm." Before Harry could start yelling again, Hermione interrupted them all. "Let us try 'magicae texentes' meaning weaving magic." "What is that?" Draco asked her. "It is a practice, though traditionally old, of forming a circle and touching the wand tips together. The magic will weave and form a single source of power, which must be controlled and targeted by the person known as the 'Caster.' Hopefully, this should work." "Hermione, are you absolutely sure about this?" Ron was a bit nervous. "If 'The Caster' doesn't direct the command thoroughly, it might end up backfiring on us again, and we all will be drenched again." "Well, Ron this is the only choice we have, until we think of something." Neville murmured. "Alright. Let us try again." Harry sighed. They formed a circle again and raised their wands towards the ceiling, so that the tips touched together. "Who'll be the Caster?" Ginny voiced out the question. "Since, Hermione gave the idea. It is only fair that she is the Caster." Harry declared. Hermione took a deep breath. "Instead of trying 'Aguamenti,' let us try 'Extinguisho.' Wands at the ready everyone." Harry sighed. He prayed silently that this worked out. If it didn't, they had no other choice but to be escorted to hell by the flames, and they would never find out the true identity of the Chosen One, exposing the world to danger.

Chapter-21---

“Go!” Hermione shrieked. “Extinguisho!’ they all uttered. A pale white string of magic emerged from each of their wands and formed a swirl above their heads. It was fascinating to look at, the magnificent white swirls with hues of blue brightened the room. Everyone turned to look at Hermione. She was sweating profusely, and her eyes were closes, she kept mumbling something to herself. Her body went rigid and her eyebrows were quivering. Ron raised to put his hand on her shoulder, but Ginny pulled it back and glared at him. Her hands were balled into fists. Hermione was trying really hard to control the force of the magic. Neville looked anxiously at Harry while Draco was fidgeting with his fingers. Suddenly, Hermione’s eyes flew open, and she yelled “Voluntaris!.” The swirl of white and blue began moving towards the flames. Harry silently hoped that this would work out. The swirl began gathering speed as it moved towards the flame, but as soon as it had a minute contact with the spark, it extinguished plunging them into darkness. “This is hopeless” Draco murmured. Hermione looked as if she was about to cry. Harry bent on his knees, defeated. There was nothing there could do now. He looked towards the wall facing him on his right. Tears began to blur his vision; his eyes fell upon the inscriptions carved on the pillar. Using his sleeves, he wiped his tears and focused on the carving. It looked like the same language which Ginny had decoded earlier. “Ginny” he called out to her. She came running towards him. “Isn’t this the same language which you had read outside. What was its name again?” “Eryndal” she murmured “Harry you are right. There is something inscribed in Eryndal.” “Well, go on and read it.” Harry insisted. She went closer to the pillar and gently traced the carvings on it. “Magic grows stronger when emotions align. Teamwork and sacrifice are three key elements of this task. But only the powerful can succeed and not the powerless ” “But what does it mean?” Neville enquired. “Even I don’t quite get it” Hermione stated. “I got it!” Ginny shrieked. “What is it?!” Harry practically yelled. “Magic grows stronger when emotions align which means that all of us have to think about an emotion together. Since this trial is about teamwork, we focus on it but I didn’t understand about the powerful and powerless thing. “Right” interrupted Hermione “Ginny’s absolutely right. The powerful and powerless thing indicates ability. Ability to withstand magic in its greatest form.” “So, you are trying to say, that whoever can withstand magic in the most resilient manner, should participate in this.” Draco began pacing around the chamber. “Exactly” Harry got up “So Ginny won’t be a part of this.” She swiftly turned to look at Harry, her face red and eyes raging. “And why I should not be a part of this?” “Because you are the youngest over here. All of us have witnessed much brutal forms of magic and fought it as well." "But I know the most perilous spells which will cause effects that you might have not even imagined in your wildest dreams" her eyes red, matching with the fiery of the flame. "I think Harry's right" Ron voiced out his opinion. "You are too young for this" Ginny glared at him. "I agree as well" Hermione and Draco said. Everyone looked at Neville for his opinion. He shrugged casually and said, "I am okay with anything." "Fine then" she huffed "But I get to reach and claim the Codex." "That is alright. After we have suppressed the flame, you can go and reach for it." Harry said. She went and sat on a stone watching them all. "Now the five of us have to concentrate extremely hard" Hermione gestured to form a circle. "Especially Neville. Concentrate on Teamwork everyone." Neville nodded. Draco and Ron looked uncertain. Harry was the only one who looked confident about this. "Point your wands towards the flame" Harry commanded. "To the count of three" Draco began counting. "One... Two.... Three!" All five of them closed their eyes and gripped their wand tightly. Each one concentrating on teamwork and friendship. Harry was concentrating on the first moment, he met Ron and Hermione on the Hogwarts Express and how they never left his side ever since. Everyone's eyes were closed, but their minds were hard at work. Neville began trembling. Draco held his wand tighter than ever. A thin stream of orangish-red shot out from their wands but disappeared quickly. Everyone opened their eyes. "It worked" Ron screeched "Did you see that?" "Yes, yes, we all did. Draco what is the matter with you?" Harry looked at him. The wand was beginning to slip from his hands, he was sweating, and his eyes were still shut. "Draco" Harry went to him "What's the matter?" Draco began weeping. Ron patted him while Harry assured him. "I-I-I c-ca-can't think of a happy memory. It is just..." Harry interrupted him. "Draco, it is not compulsory to think about the past, you can even focus on the present, where we are now, we are together. Draco nodded. "It doesn't matter what we were before, it is about what we are now." "Neville, what's the matter with you?" Ron interrupted him. Neville looked paler than ever, his face crimson with fear. The flame raged more fiercely than ever. "I want you all to concentrate" Harry addressed everyone "Please. Try to concentrate. I know its difficult, but let's do it." Hermione and Ron nodded. Draco regained his composure and looked solemn. Neville looked down at the floor. They formed the circle again and raised their wands. Harry eyed all of them. Ginny was sitting bored on the rock. "Go!" Hermione said and they began concentrating harder than ever. Draco and Neville looked firm while Hermione and Ron were straining themselves. They were different from each other, but at this moment, their minds were the same, analyzing every occasion they had spent together. After several seconds, of firm focus and concentration, the stream of orangish-red shot out from their wands. No one dared to lose concentration, the stream flew into the air, crossed the line, and began floating towards the flame. At first, it looked like the stream of orange and red had abruptly halted due to lack of concentration, but the flow of the spell didn't falter. It kept drifting in the direction of the flame and ultimately, touched the flame. All five of them opened their eyes but didn't lower their wands. The spurt from their wands spread throughout the flame from a sole source of magic ahead of it. The flames slowly began to extinguish, thus becoming steady and calm. "Ginny. Go ahead and take it quick." Harry barked. Ginny swiftly walked towards the flame; the Codex began to glow bright with every step she took. She was radiating the same glow which the Codex had. Ginny walked towards the pedestal. The chamber became so silent, as if witnessing the entire scene. The Codex began to pulse like a heart. Her eyes were gleaming in the darkness of the chamber. Every strand of her hair began to sparkle like the stars. She stepped in front of the pedestal. The Codex threatened to explode the light it contained. The light from the Codex was comparatively dull, than the light which illuminated from her body. She gently reached towards the Codex and touched it. The moment she touched, its light erupted. It wasn't gentle- it was a storm. The stone slabs began crumbling beneath her feet. Strings of the Pyrope garnet spread from the Codex, as soon as she touched it, the strings wound themselves round her wrist and spread throughout her body. The air was thick with spells. Ginny floated mid-air as the strings from the Codex wound around her entire body. . Her friends watched awed and were unable to utter any word. Power pressed against her chest, and the resolve began to crumble. The magic that slept through ages, recognized only her. She stood bathed in power, a halo of flame, a deity of light. The others flinched, but she was unyielding, determined, and focused. Nothing could stop her, nothing could break her, nothing could ever be compared to her. She was reckless, fearless, and bold. Power seeped through her veins.

The gem had chosen.

And it had chosen her.

Chapter-22----

"No!" Harry screamed on his knees. "No! It can't! It can't be her!" Ron was on the ground, supporting the wall unable to speak and frozen as if bound by a full-body-bind curse. Hermione kept looking at the floor and began pacing around mumbling to herself. Draco and Neville were on the ground trying to figure out exactly what was going on. Ginny Weasley- The Chosen One opened her eyes. Her eye color was so different from her normal light brown eyes. Now, it was slowly turning light grey. The length of her hair began decreasing until her shoulders and the color changed from bright red to whitish-blond. The freckles on her face began to decrease and gradually disappeared. Her face structure changed into a pale pointed face. At that moment, Draco finally got up from the ground. He was thrown onto the ground by the dazzling light which had emerged when Ginny had touched the Codex. He looked at the scene unfold in front of him and his eyes began to bulge inside his head. His breathing began rapidly; his heartbeat echoed throughout the entire room. His whole body began trembling. As her hair flickered, he thought it was a trick of the light. But as he saw the features shift- a young girl, younger than him and resembled the mirror image of Draco in feminine form. The shape of her face, the incline of her jaw, the unmistakable smile that he had seen in the mirror too many times- it was her. A walking corpse, an illusion, a phantom made to misled, the tricks played by his subconscious mind. He was imagining her. The room tilted, as the truth burdened his shoulders, the guilt began to eat away his internals, making him lose his balance. He supported a nearby rock. With the last bit of composure he had he murmured "D-D-Drea?" a whisper which was inaudible. The creepers on the wall moved a bit close as if trying to hear the name form on his lips. Ginny nodded. He crumpled onto the floor. Not caring about the eyes eyeing him. He began writhing and screaming on the floor as if hit by a Cruciatus curse. His hands flew to his ears, only to hide her laugh, her voice which he had ached to hear after he had discovered about her. Discovered. It was a strange but curious word. He had learnt about her a few days ago as an abandoned child, most likely to be a dead corpse and here she was. Right ahead of him. Ten steps separated him from his sister. Sister. The word seems so foreign and unknown to him. Drea began laughing. Her laughter was exactly like his. She was Draco in feminine form and more attractive. A small smile tugged at her cheeks, exposing her dimples. "Very weak, you are" she paused for a moment before using the endearment term that tied her to him, which tethered their lives forever. "Brother." "I expected something more from you. Yet you are so weak, so fragile, so selfish. Just like father. "Draco was still weeping on the floor. He had exhausted himself and barely contained any tears. Seeing no response, she continued "I was barely a year old, when our dear father left me in Knockturn Alley. He was ashamed. Ashamed of having a girl child in the family. But I managed to survive alright. Every second, every day I dreamt of having a happy life with my family. But no. My family considered me to be dead. A dead corpse. I survived, I learnt. Learned the most brutal spells and how to conjure them. Being an avid reader, I used to sneak to Diagon Alley, and steal books from the shops. From there, I learnt and researched throughout the years. I even learnt new languages." "But why did you want the Codex?" Hermione mustered her courage to speak. "Shut up! YOU FILTHY LITTLE MUDBLOOD!" Drea shrieked. Ron took a few steps towards her. "Don't you dare." She pointed her finger towards him "I wanted the Codex as I already knew I was The Chosen one. Not going to reveal all my secrets, but once I knew it, I decided to retrieve the Codex, to harness the power within it and have control over the world. But there is a slight problem. To fully harness and control the powers of all three Codex, I need to sacrifice." She paused, looking around at their petrified faces. "I need a sacrifice. Only then, will the power be mine and I will control this world and rid it of Mudbloods.." Draco was still frozen. His mind seemed to betray him. He was imagining things. "Why" he paused for breath and weeping in the middle "Why did you become evil?" "Evil?!" she laughed. "My dear brother. This isn't about evil or good. It is about power. The one who has it will be the supreme. I have spent my days in horrible conditions, begging for food and shelter. Power is a kind of addiction- which seems to make everyone blind." "Where is Ginny?!" Ron yelled at her. "Lower your tone. Your sister is fine. She is kept somewhere safe and hidden. Enough waste of time. I need a sacrifice." She pointed her finger at Draco and smiled. Her eyes were consumed with thirst for power and ability. Draco pleaded with her with his eyes. He was too broken, too lost to speak. Ignored by a mother, Forced by a father, and now killed by a sister. Drea smiled and said, "Sweet Dreams, Brother" With that, she snapped her fingers. The glow condensed into a spiral, threads of Draco's soul unwinding from his body and coiling upward into Drea's outstretched hand. The chamber howled as if mourning what was going on. His face twisted between terror and agony, then slackened as the last fragment of light wrenched itself loose. And then silence. His body collapsed to the ground like a discarded shell, empty, motionless. The final parts of his soul bled into Drea's grasp. The chamber bowed to her fury, and the others lay broken in the shadows, powerless to stop what she had become...